Returning her attention back to the fire, Stormy saw that most of their bus was now engulfed in flames and the smoke was growing ever thicker. The wind had picked up, lapping at the flames, blowing the smoke further down the road. In a momentary gap in the heavy smoke, she caught a quick glimpse of a shadowy figure standing on the far side of the road. From what she could make out, it appeared to be intently scanning the crowd of passengers. Then the smoke closed in around the bus as quickly as it had parted, masking the figure from sight. With the next gust of wind, the smoke parted once more and the figure was gone.

The Austin Fires

A Stormy Winters Mystery

S. A. Slack

authorHOUSE®

AuthorHouse™
1663 Liberty Drive, Suite 200
Bloomington, IN 47403
www.authorhouse.com
Phone: 1-800-839-8640

© 2007 S. A. Slack. All rights reserved.

No part of this book may be reproduced, stored in a retrieval system, or transmitted by any means without the written permission of the author.

First published by AuthorHouse 9/12/2007

ISBN: 978-1-4343-2582-2 (sc)

Library of Congress Control Number: 2007905636

Printed in the United States of America
Bloomington, Indiana

This book is printed on acid-free paper.

For my parents, Stormy and Larry, and my husband,
Edwin, thanks for all of your help and encouragement.

Chapter One

The landing gear of the 747 dropped smoothly into place beneath its large shining silver belly. The wing's spoilers were lowered, airbrakes applied, and the deep black asphalt of the runway appeared ever closer preparatory to its landing at the Dallas/Fort Worth International Airport. Inside, over the heads of the waiting passengers, the 'fasten seat belt' signs glowed and a co-pilots' friendly voice sounded over the intercom welcoming them to the Great State of Texas and wishing them a very pleasant stay.

"We've arrived," Stormy said, elbowing her husband, Lance, in the ribs. "Put your book away."

"Almost finished," Lance replied, turning a page.

It had been a relaxing few hours for Stormy Winters as she sat near the window along side her husband. She would have enjoyed the flight much more if not for the seats being so cramped for space that she could not fully stretch out her legs. In an attempt to make things a little more comfortable, Lance had stretched one of his long legs out into the aisle, running it along the seat in front of him as close as he could manage. The space was so limited that Stormy had worried that if the passenger in front of her reclined his seat back any farther, he would have been lying in her lap and snoring up her nostrils.

Hopefully he doesn't have bad breath, she thought.

In consideration for the passenger behind her, she had been careful not to lean her own seat back very far.

Stormy had just celebrated her 65th birthday, though she didn't look a day over 50, surprising many, when on occasion she would reveal her true age. Smooth skin and lovely blue-gray eyes, framed by dark-blonde hair combed neatly into place, may have attributed to this misconception. Lightly applied make-up adorned her face, as she refused to pile it on like ladies of the evening, and a light scent of roses floated throughout the air about her. The tailored blue-and-peach-flowered shirt and light blue pants fit her ever so nicely, accented by a pair of navy opened-toed sandals. She rarely ever wore closed-toed shoes, claiming they were too hot and uncomfortable.

Lance, at 67, looked more his age with his short graying hair, nicely groomed salt and pepper mustache, and the wisdom of the years reflecting forth from soft brown eyes. It was often said, much to his chagrin, that he had 'robbed the cradle' when he married Stormy. For this trip, he'd chosen to wear a green button-down shirt and tan slacks. They hung quite nicely on his tall frame and his black loafers sported a spit-polished shine. His tanned skin was the result of his many hours spent beneath the hot Arizona sun caring for his prized rose garden. One only had to look at Lance to notice the fine

The Austin Fires

military bearing about him from his many years of service in the U S Army.

For retired people, Stormy and Lance found themselves always on the go. There were doctor appointments to keep, sales promotions to check out, church functions to attend, relative's birthday parties to go to, sick friends to visit in the hospital and a million and one other things to keep their days full. When the chance had come up for them to go on a tour of Austin, Texas, Stormy was delighted. Just the month before, her friend, Ardeth had stopped her in the church hallway after services and raved about the good time she and her daughter had experienced on their trip to the southern states, including the historical city of Austin. Lance had not needed much prodding to agree to this trip when she had showed him the tour's brochure. As they prepared to leave, their house had been filled with much anticipation at all the fun and excitement of seeing new places and different things this trip held.

As the planes wheels touched down on the runway, Stormy thought back over their flight. When they had boarded the plane in Phoenix, Lance insisted that Stormy take the seat by the window as he knew she enjoyed looking out at the passing scenery as they flew along. Indeed, she had watched most of their progress from the deserts around Phoenix to the plains of the Dallas/ Ft. Worth area.

Along the way, she had taken note of many interesting things below them, as well as in the skies above. Through her window, she had spied an assortment of various shaped clouds, some hanging in thick, menacing layers, while others were just a thin wisp of white against a field of blue. Several clouds had floated by her window like the large balloons passing down the avenue in a Macy's parade on Thanksgiving morning, casting their shadows on the landscape below. Others had appeared to be chasing one another throughout the sky in a race to see which would be the first to arrive at some distant mountain beyond.

She had spotted large circles of hay fields that dotted the ground below, many forming complete circles, while others looked like some one had cut them in half. Some fields formed of three-quarter circles had Stormy chuckling, reminding her of a large 'Pac man' ready to munch the other circles right up. The larger rectangular patches of the hay fields reminded her of green covered ping-pong tables waiting for players to start a game upon their velvety surfaces. She had observed roads that stretched on for miles over the desert sands, looking quite lonely with only a few cars or trucks traveling upon them. It made the world below look very empty indeed!

Stormy had marveled at cracks that ran in groups across the land, like flowing veins showing through the earth's skin, while low mountain ranges had reminded her of pie crust edges hastily pinched into place by some giant hand. Small communities had come and gone in the blink of an eye, while others were laid out in the pattern of large computer motherboards. Best of all, she had witnessed huge patches of red and beige earth spread out into an amazing mosaic of a Chinese dragon. She had quickly snapped a few photos from the plan window as proof to her friend's that she was not making this up when she described her trip for them upon returning home.

Stormy had been surprised at how beautiful and green the area around Dallas was. Compared to the dry deserts of Arizona, it was a virtual paradise. Lakes, rivers,

The Austin Fires

and swimming pools dotted the whole Dallas area. The few times she and Lance had driven through the Texas Panhandle, it had been hot, bleak, and dusty. She had expected it to be similar this time as well.

What a pleasant surprise, Stormy had thought, drinking in the scene. *Hopefully, Austin will be as nice.*

Stormy was roused from her thoughts as she noticed that several of her fellow passengers had unfastened their seatbelts and were gathering up their belongings.

"Well, that was a short flight," Lance said, arising from his seat and reaching for their carry-ons in the overhead bin above them.

"Only because you had your nose in that Sci-fi book the whole way," Stormy replied. She retrieved her dark brown walking stick as she rose to her feet, a one-inch copper kokopeli dangling from the black leather strap near its top.

She found her stick to be quite useful whenever she had to walk long distances or when navigating difficult areas, as she limped ever so slightly due to an operation on her hip a few years back. It came in handy for other things as well, such as the sandals she had recently pulled down from the stores top shelf when she had found no salesperson around to assist her.

Why should I wait thirty minutes for assistance when I can have them down in two, she had reasoned to herself.

Taking the small flowered travel bag Lance handed to her, and placing it in one hand, she threw her black leather purse over the opposite shoulder and started down the narrow isle balancing carefully with her stick.

"He's a pretty good writer, you know," Lance defended the author, tucking the book into the side pocket of his laptop case and following after her. "I wanted to finish it before we landed."

"Well, I guess it kept you busy anyway," Stormy chuckled.

Stepping through the plane's exit door, they followed the long enclosed ramp down and out into the airport's terminal. Making their way through the crowds of passengers waiting to board the next flights out, they headed for the restroom area. The rest of their tour group would be joining them for next flight, as they were all coming from other areas of the country and would meet for the tour's flight to Austin here at the Dallas/Fort Worth airport.

"Why don't we get something to eat?" Lance suggested, as Stormy rejoined him outside the entrance to the restrooms. "We have a few hours to kill before our flight to Austin."

"Sounds good to me," Stormy said. "I'm starving. How about some burgers? The food smells absolutely delicious coming from that place over there," she said, pointing in the direction of a small, colorful café.` Lively western music spilled forth from its entrance.

"Lead the way," Lance said, following behind her while dodging the passengers, hurrying to make their departing flights.

After being seated at a cozy table for two by an attractive waitress dressed in a short turquoise western skirt and white frilly blouse, they both ordered huge hamburger plates which came with mounds of sizzling golden french-fries and side orders of creamy coleslaw. The food turned out to taste as good as it smelled though the portions were a little more than Stormy could eat at one sitting. Normally at home she would ask for a take out box, but since they had to catch another flight she would forgo it this time. She couldn't resist, however, one small bite of the strawberry-covered cheesecake that Lance had ordered. Stormy marveled at Lance, for no matter what he ate, he always seemed to have room for dessert somehow.

With satisfied stomachs, they paid their bill including a generous tip. Having some time before their flight left, the two leisurely strolled around the crowded terminal looking through the various shop entrances at the many souvenirs and trinkets for sale. They spotted all kinds of interesting items through out the shops, but nothing so far that really appealed or called out to them "buy me".

"Look at that, Lance," Stormy exclaimed, pointing to a display of charms hanging in the window of a small shop they were approaching. "Wouldn't that look great on my stick? It would add a little more pizzazz to it, don't you think."

"Well, I guess it could use a little more help, now that you mention it," Lance replied, a grin spreading across his handsome face.

"Come on," Stormy sighed, heading for the door to have a closer look.

Lance followed, and soon they were holding up the various charms against Stormy's stick in an attempt to choose one that she felt would go well with her cooper kokopeli.

"I think this one will do quite nicely," Stormy said, holding up a small finely carved wooden buffalo head from the display. "I have always loved buffalos, and this one will look great with the kokopeli."

"Well at least it won't add any more weight to your luggage," Lance teased her, as he handed money over to the cashier.

"No, I don't think there'll be a problem with that," Stormy laughed, tucking the small brown bag safely into her purse as they left the shop.

Each of them had saved extra room in their luggage for souvenirs of their trip to Texas. They had not planned things as well on previous trips, and they had lived to regret it, usually having to purchase a new suitcase for the added treasures they had found along the way. This time they were better prepared, they hoped.

They wandered in and out of a few more of the shops, and though they saw many other interesting items, they found nothing either of them really needed. They were in a small bookshop when Lance came over to Stormy, touching her arm and startling her as she was bent over to take a closer look at a row of gum, candy, and breathe mints.

"We had better get to our next flight, Storm," Lance said, checking his silver and gold wristwatch, "and check in with our group."

"Okay. Just let me pay for these mints and grab a bottle of water for each of us," she replied, removing the wallet from her purse.

They headed off toward the next flights' waiting area a few minutes ahead of the scheduled meeting time. They were looking forward to seeing who they would be traveling with to Austin. While Stormy enjoyed meeting new people, Lance wasn't always so positive about this.

As they approached the gate, they noticed a short, balding pale-skinned man with wire-framed glasses

The Austin Fires

standing by a sign that read "Texas' Great Tours--Austin". He wore a tan western shirt tucked into dark blue jeans that were held up by a brown leather belt. A huge silver buckle hung at his waist and a pair of newly polished black boots adorned his feet. He held a fawn-colored Stetson in one hand and a sheaf of papers in the other. A few people were crowded around him, involved in an excited conversation.

"I guess that's our group over there," Stormy said, pointing with her walking stick at the group ahead.

"It looks like it," Lance said, heading that way.

Chapter Two

"Ah, Mr. and Mrs. Winters, I presume. Welcome to Texas," said the guide in a deep Texas drawl. "I'm Clint Black, no relation to the singer, and I'll be your guide for the next few days. I hope you received your packet of information that was sent out to you last month. I have a few more papers and a nametag for each of you. Make sure you wear your tag at all times so we'll get acquainted more easily."

He handed them each a stack of papers and several brochures, including a tag in the shape of a star with their names plainly written upon it. The look that Lance flashed Stormy clearly showed his disapproval of the tag, but she knew he would quietly go along with it.

Clint introduced them to the two couples standing nearby, each person wearing a nametag on their shirts. The guide explained that the fifth pair, who were coming from Chicago to accompany them on the tour, had had to cancel at the last minute due to illness.

"It will just be eight of you I'll have the pleasure of guiding around Austin this time out," Clint said. "Now excuse me folks while I go in search of the last pair on our tour before they start the boarding procedures," Off he dashed into the crowd.

Mr. and Mrs. Thornton look like a nice enough couple, though Mr. Thornton appears to be a little deaf as he talks rather loudly, thought Stormy, as the couple discussed something between themselves.

They both appeared to be in their mid-seventies. Mr. Thornton was totally bald, and wore dark blue suspenders to hold up his navy blue pants, with a crisp white dress shirt tucked underneath them. Mrs. Thornton seemed to be rather on the shy side and much quieter than her husband. She wore a nice pants outfit of deep purple, with matching shoes, and carried a large tapestry purse which seemed to hold everything they might need for the trip, and more. She demonstrated this as she searched through the deep recesses of her bag and pulled out a rather large magnifying glass.

"Here you are, Frank," she said, handing it over to her husband. He held it up before him so he could have a better look at the words on the paper he was holding. "Please just call us Frank and Nancy. We're from Atlanta. That's in Georgia you know," she told the rest of the group.

The other two introduced themselves as sisters, Kim Smith and Kati Giles, from Colorado Springs, Colorado. Both appeared to be in their late forties. They remarked that their last children, both boys, had just graduated from high school that spring and were off together at the University of Colorado. The sisters had decided it was

The Austin Fires

about time they got out and saw more of this big country in which they lived.

"We left our husbands at home to fend for themselves," Kati said, laughing. "We were tired of waiting until they retired from their jobs "some day", and they couldn't get the time off right now to accompany us on this trip."

"So here we are," Kim chimed in, smiling.

Stormy smiled back as she surveyed the sister's matching dark black jeans and bright red t-shirts with the word 'Sisters' across the front of them in bold cursive writing. The two sisters looked so much alike that no one could have mistaken that they were related. Both appeared so full of energy and excitement that Stormy could not help but be glad to have them along on the tour.

"Would you take a few pictures of us here in the airport before we board?" Kim asked Stormy, handing her a small camera.

"We are keeping a travel log of our trip to show the family back home in Colorado," Kim explained.

"I'd love to. Where do you want to stand?" Stormy asked, handing her walking stick over to Lance as she examined the digital camera closely. The two sisters stood next to the airline desk with the boarding gate behind them. The sign above the gate showed the flight that would be taking them to Austin, with the flight number and its time of departure. Stormy snapped a few pictures of the brightly smiling duo.

"You both photograph very well," she said to them.

"Thanks," the sisters said in unison.

"We will now be boarding for flight 918 to Austin. Have your boarding passes ready, please," a pleasant sounding female voice announced over the loud speaker. "We will start with anyone in wheelchairs or with walkers first, and then those with small babies and children. Please come forward now."

"I guess we'll have to wait a few minutes. My ticket says we're in 'Group 4'," said Kati, showing it to her sister, Kim.

"Looks like we're all in that group, young lady," said Frank, a bit too loudly.

At that moment, Clint came rushing up with a young man and woman in tow. The two looked to be in their mid-twenties, a deep scowl showing across the young man's face making him look rather unpleasant.

The two were both fit looking, as if they worked out each day at the gym. The man's jet-black hair hung part way over his piercing deep brown eyes. He wore dark jeans and a black short sleeved t-shirt with a picture of a man surfing his way across the front of it. Clean white sneakers completed his look, which choice Stormy found a little odd considering the dark color of the rest of his clothes. He was handsome in a rugged sort of way.

The man's companion was shorter, with shoulder length red hair. She was dressed in tightly fitting dark blue jeans and an emerald green blouse, with dark green sandals to match. She looked lively and excited about the trip, though appearing a little nervous at the same time.

"Here we are, and just in time for boarding I see," Clint said, as group number four was asked to board over the loud speaker. "This is Tom Peters and Amy Jensen," he said, hurriedly introducing them to the others. "Well, let's get aboard, y'all and get this tour rolling."

The Austin Fires

They boarded the flight, found their assigned seats, and got settled in. Flight attendants in navy blue pants and light blue short-sleeved shirts came around offering them small pillows and light blue blankets for the flight. They told the passengers that they would be serving beverages and snacks later on during the flight.

"Fasten your seat belts, and have your seats in the upright position,' a beautiful long haired stewardess announced over the loud speaker from the front of the cabin area. "Please turn off all of your electronic devices, such as your laptops and game boys. You will be able to turn them back on once we have reached our cruising altitude."

"Looks like an interesting bunch we have on the tour with us," Lance whispered to Stormy, fluffing his pillow and placing it behind his head.

"Yes, my thoughts exactly," she returned. "I'm sure they will be okay once we get to know them better. I can hardly wait to see the sights of Austin."

Stormy once again sat in the window seat and enjoyed looking down out of the plane's window at the scenery below her. With each passing mile, the area filled in with more and more trees, green grass, lakes and several blue pools.

After a time, it became much too dark to see any of the area below except for the lights of farmhouses and other buildings. She turned on the overhead light and aimed it at her seat so as not to disturb Lance. He had become tired and was sleeping beside her. She took a new paperback mystery novel from her purse which had been written by one of her favorite authors, and sat back

S. A. Slack

to read for the remainder of the flight. Oh, how she loved a good mystery!

Soon they were landing in Austin, and once again Lance retrieved their things from the overhead compartment. They were hustled off to the luggage carousel, and it seemed to take forever before the red light started to flash. One by one, the suitcases appeared and fell onto the turning conveyor belt below. Around and around they went, awaiting their owner's attention and retrieval.

It's always a gamble, Stormy thought, *to check ones' luggage with the airlines. Who knows if our luggage will arrive at the same time we do, or be sent off to who knows where for who knows how long.*

Luckily, at that moment, Stormy spotted her bright blue suitcase and Lance's large green one coming around the far corner of the carousel. Lance reached out as the luggage came near them and grabbed the two, setting them on the floor beside him. Glancing around the room, Stormy noticed that the others in their group had also managed to locate their own bags as well.

The tour guide waved to them from across the carousel, and beckoned them over to a place by him along side a nearby bench.

"From here we will take a bus into town to our hotel," Clint said. "Please follow me." He turned and headed for the nearest door of the terminal, the group following along behind.

Once outside, a cool breeze blew gently across Stormy's face as they walked across the pavement.

"This feels nice after being cooped up in that stuffy plane," Stormy said, looking around her and enjoying the evening air.

"Yes, I agree with you there," Lance replied, pulling his green suitcase behind him as they walked side by side.

They boarded a large bus parked along a yellow painted curb with the rest of the group and stored their luggage in the racks provided for such items. It was already crowded with other passengers, but Stormy and Lance managed to find a couple of seats near the back of the bus. Stormy disliked sitting in the back of a bus, the fumes bothering her sensitive nose, but there was no other choice on this run. She took out a tissue from her purse just in case.

Chapter Three

A few moments later, the bus departed the Burgstrom Airport and headed out to Hwy 192. They would be staying at the famed Drakeson Hotel. Stormy and Lance had looked it up on the internet and found it had been built in the late 1800's by a rich Texas rancher. It was a little on the pricey side, but they were both looking forward to staying there.

After several miles, they merged onto Hwy 35, and Stormy noticed the smell of smoke drifting back toward them in the rear of the bus.

It is probably just someone's fireplace burning, she thought, *though it really isn't all that cold out this time of the year.*

After a few more minutes had past, the smell of smoke became much stronger. This alarmed Stormy even further.

"Lance, do you smell smoke?" Stormy asked, taking in another whiff of the air around them.

"Yes, now that you mention it I do," he said. "It smells like oil of some kind is burning."

A woman's loud scream echoed through the bus, causing them to look several seats up toward the front of the bus. The young woman was Amy, and she was out of her seat, shouting at the bus driver. The driver swerved past a slowly moving car and quickly pulled the large bus over to the side of the highway.

Smoke was filling the inside of the bus, causing many of the passengers to choke and cough. Stormy's eyes filled with tears, making it hard for her to see much of anything past the seat where they were sitting. Several of the men sitting near them, with the help of Lance, had opened the back door of the bus and were throwing luggage out of the way onto the side of the road as fast as they could. Next, they helped the few passengers who were in the back down from the bus. Lance lowered Stormy quickly to the ground and steered her away from the bus. He hurried back to see if he could be of help to anyone else.

Looking around the back end of the bus, Stormy saw that several passengers had already exited from the front door and were making their way onto the road's dirt shoulder and away from the smoke.

The driver ushered them into the nearby trees and away from the bus, now burning from its middle section. The hungry flames leapt into the air in bright reds, yellows, and oranges as thick black smoke poured out of the open windows and up from the belly of the bus.

The passengers spread out into groups, staring wide-eyed at the flames as sirens sounded in the distance. Clint double checked with all those in his tour group and made

The Austin Fires

sure there were no injures that needed tending to. The luggage, piled nearby, would have to be sorted out later.

"Are you alright my dear?" Lance asked, coming over to Stormy and putting his arm around her shoulders. "That was a close one. It could have been worse though."

"Yes, I'm fine. A little shook up, but I'm okay," she replied, looking down at the hand he held up next to his soot-covered shirt. "What about you? How'd you get that cut on your hand?"

Stormy gently took his injured hand in hers, and taking a tissue from out of her pocket, pressed it against the wound.

"It happened when we were tossing the luggage from the bus so quickly. It'll be okay," Lance said, thankful once again for being married to such a kind woman as Stormy was.

"I'll look at it closer when we get to the hotel," Stormy said, hugging Lance a little tighter.

Returning her attention back to the fire, she saw that most of their bus was now engulfed in flames, and the smoke was growing ever thicker. The wind had picked up and was lapping at the flames, blowing the smoke further down the road. There was a momentary gap in the heavy smoke as the wind blew it aside from the surrounding area. Stormy caught a quick glimpse of a shadowy figure standing on the far side of the road. From what she could see, it appeared to be a man intently scanning the crowd of passengers. Then the smoke closed in around the bus as quickly as it had parted, masking the figure from sight. With the next gust of wind, the smoke parted once more and the figure was gone.

"That was weird," Stormy mused.

"What was that?" Lance said, turning in her direction. He had been in conversation with their tour guide, Clint. Now Clint moved in the direction of where the sisters stood presumably to check on them.

"Nothing," she said, as the fire trucks roared to a stop near the burning bus. "What was Clint saying?"

"He said that the driver had gotten in touch with the bus company, and that they are sending out another bus as soon as possible. It will take at least thirty to forty minutes for it to arrive though. Why don't we sit down on our luggage while we wait?" he suggested. Lance took Stormy by her arm and guided her to the pile of luggage.

As they sat there, more emergency vehicles arrived. Stormy looked around at the others in their tour group. Frank was talking with Clint, and seemed to be directing him in what he thought Clint should be doing. Clint patiently listened, but looked a little annoyed at the same time. Frank's wife, Nancy, had found her own luggage and was sitting quietly off to the side, searching for something in that big purse of hers.

On the other side of Nancy, Stormy saw that Kim and Kati were busy searching through the pile of luggage for their own cases. Or were they? She saw Kati glance around at the group, then quickly pick up a small red bag and start to carry it off. Kim, noticing her sister's actions, said something Stormy couldn't quite make out. This caused Kati to throw the case back onto the pile of discarded luggage and move away from it. Kati looked around at the group once more and then walked over to where Kim was retrieving a large black suitcase. The sisters whispered together for a few moments, then Kim

The Austin Fires

looked around at the group and spying Stormy looking their way, smiled and pointed out to Kati another large black suitcase. Kati seemed to feign surprise and moved over to the case, which she quickly retrieved and pulled back to where her sister stood.

Those two sure are acting odd, Stormy thought. *You'd think that Kati would know what suitcase she'd brought with her.*

Just beyond the sisters, Tom stood scowling at the fire, hands buried deep in the front pockets of his jeans. Amy, standing next to him, spoke a few words in his direction. He did not respond to whatever she had said, so with a shake of her red hair, she turned toward the luggage. She looked up and noticed Stormy looking her way. She flashed her a quick smile and continued to walk toward the pile of luggage.

"I wonder what their story is?" Stormy said. "They don't seem to click too well together".

"I don't know," Lance replied, looking over at Tom. "You know how some of these young college types are these days. They're always moping around if they don't get their way or are inconvenienced in some how."

"Yes, I've seen that in alot of people these days," she agreed.

Several police cars arrived on the scene and two uniformed officers made their way throughout the crowd asking many questions. They inquired of each person what they had seen concerning the fire and if they had any ideas of how it may have started.

Stormy had little information to contribute to their investigation, other than the fact of smelling smoke a short while before the bus had pulled over to the side of the road. She thought it better not to mention the shadowy figure she had seen earlier. It was probably just a curiosity seeker anyway.

The new replacement bus finally arrived and everyone was herded on board it. Several of the men, including Lance, reloaded the pile of luggage and they were once again on their way. The passengers were tired, and most of them sat quietly back in their seats for the rest of the ride to the hotel.

Chapter Four

When they arrived at the Drakeston Hotel, the bus driver announced over the intercom that they had arranged with the hotel's manager for them to enjoy a great dinner in the hotel's restaurant, compliments of the bus company. This perked up the group as they arose from their seats and gathered up their personal items.

"Please enjoy your stay here in Austin, capital of the great state of Texas," the driver continued, helping the passengers to disembark. "Check at the hotel's registration desk for brochures and schedules. There's plenty to do and see here in Austin."

"We've got plenty of things planned for you folks," Clint said, after they got their luggage and were assembled on the sidewalk in front of the hotel. "Come with me and we'll get you checked into your rooms first."

Stormy looked up at the hotel's outer Victorian styling. It was every bit as gorgeous as the brochure said it would be. Its four stories were built of beautifully carved blocks of solid looking light grey granite with intricately cut arches over each of its windows and doors. Several gables, balconies, and bends graced its front walls which made it an intriguing and beautiful sight. The windows were ablaze with bright lights, and old-fashioned lamplights adorned both sides of the hotel's front entrance, two huge solid oak doors. She wondered what it might have been like when it was first built back in the 1800's.

It was most likely lit entirely with street lamps outside and candles or oil lamps within. she thought. *How romantic it must have been back then.* She always enjoyed historical places.

Two bellhops rolled the luggage behind the group on a large cart as they entered the hotel's lobby, where a man dressed in a well-tailored navy blue suit approached them in greeting. He conversed a moment with Clint and then beckoned the group to follow him. Turning, he headed across the lobby toward a large desk.

"This is absolutely beautiful," Stormy said, studying each wall of the lobby as they crossed its wide expanse. "Look at all these fine sculptures and the wonderful woven rugs and paintings on the walls. It reminds me of being in a museum."

"Yes, it is very nice. It should be for the amount we paid to stay here," Lance reminded her. "But I guess it's about time we stayed some where else besides the Motel Six."

"I guess so," Stormy said, laughing.

After they had registered and had been given their room keys, a young woman dressed in a navy blue pants suit led the group to the elevators in what was called the

Old Wing. The group crowded into one of the elevators, while the bellhops with their luggage got into another.

Arriving at their floor, they stepped out into a richly decorated hallway. A deep blue and gold rug had been rolled down the hall's center over plush beige carpeting. Various paintings hung on the walls at regular intervals throughout and small tables, set here and there against the walls, held elegant vases containing fresh cut roses, carnations, and other colorful flowers. Most of them had been given rooms close to each other, with the exception of Tom and Clint, who had rooms at the far end of the floor. A young bellhop unlocked the doors to their rooms for them, each in turn, stating that if they needed anything to give them a ring.

Stepping into the room, Stormy caught her breath.

"Wow! This is fantastic, Lance," she said, taking it all in. "Look at this room."

"Pretty nice indeed," he remarked, looking around in admiration.

A king-sized bed, draped in a beautiful quilt of deep browns and rich golds, accented by several golden throw pillows, sat against a far wall. Over-sized deep golden-colored velvet drapes surrounded a tall pair of white French doors which led out to a balcony that overlooked the street below. Several over-stuffed cocoa-colored chairs and a few small tables were set around the spacious room, with a dark wood writing desk off to one side. Lovely scenic paintings graced the deep apricot painted walls, giving the room a finishing touch.

"Take a look at this bathroom," Lance called to Stormy from another doorway.

On entering the room, she noticed the beautiful white marble-tiled counter and back splash. The sink and over-sized bathtub, held up by four enormous claw-like legs, were adorned with shiny brass fixtures. Thick white towels hung from brass towel racks, and two heavy robes were neatly arranged on pegs near the door. They both agreed that this was the most elegant bathroom they had ever seen.

Stormy was anxious to try the bath out, but that would have to wait for later that night. They'd been instructed by their guide to settle their things into the rooms and meet the others downstairs in the Drakeston's restaurant for dinner in the next thirty minutes. She and Lance hurried to freshen up.

On leaving their room, Stormy noticed the sisters, Kim and Kati, just reaching the elevator. The doors had opened and the sisters were about to step inside.

"Hold the doors for us, please," Stormy shouted as she and Lance hurried to get there in time.

As they arrived, they found Kati holding the door open with one hand while Kim firmly pressed the elevator's door open button. Lance and Stormy stepped inside and the doors closed behind them.

"Thanks for waiting," Stormy said. "I'm starving and the sooner we get to the dining area, the sooner we can eat."

"I agree," Kim said, laughing. "We didn't have any time between our flights to stop for something to eat."

"Yes, I'm hungry, too," said Katie.

"Well here we are ladies. After you," Lance said, waiting for the three women to exit the car.

The Austin Fires

The four of them headed through the lobby and entered the restaurant. This was the famous five-star restaurant Stormy had read to Lance about from one of the brochures they had received prior to the trip.

They found each table elegantly set with white linen tablecloths, exquisite china, full settings of silverware, and beautiful golden goblets. Sconces, hanging from pillars throughout the room held glowing electrical torches, their light reflecting off mirrors placed randomly among the ceiling's titles, giving the room a romantic feeling.

The maitre d' led them to a large table at the far side of the dinning room. Already seated around it were the Thorntons and their tour guide, Clint. The sisters sat next to Clint. Stormy and Lance sat down on the opposite side of the table, leaving two empty chairs for Tom and Amy when they arrived.

"We've already placed our order, so go ahead and decide what you want to have," said Frank, his voice echoing off the nearby wall.

"Yes Sir and Madame. Let your waiter know when you are ready to order," said the maitre d'. He handed them each a menu and then excused himself with a small bow.

"Nice place, don't you think," Frank said loudly.

"Lovely," Stormy replied. "I wonder where Tom and Amy are?"

As if on cue they walked through the door and were led to the table by the maitre d'. He handed them their menus, and said their waiter would be with them shortly before excusing himself.

A moment later, a friendly waiter dressed in black pants, a crisp white long-sleeved dress shirt, black vest, and deep red bow tie approached their table. He set down the large loaf of freshly baked bread he was carrying on a silver tray with a side dish of creamy butter and promised to return in a few minutes to take their orders.

Once again, Stormy noticed how grumpy Tom was. Amy tried to smile and act as if all was right with the world.

Tom has such an angry look to him, she thought. *I wonder what makes him act that way?*

The waiter returned as promised, and they all placed their orders.

Shortly thereafter, a waitress, in an outfit similar to their waiter's, approached with a younger woman following behind. She was pushing a cart full of fresh lettuces, tomatoes, and other assorted produce along with several choices of homemade salad dressings. The waitress cut up the vegetables, and tossed the salad in a grand show of expertise. Her assistant served the salads, asking each person what kind of dressing they would like and if they would enjoy freshly ground pepper and grated cheese on top of it.

"This is a very tasty salad," Lance said.

"Best one I've had in ages," Kim agreed. "I'll have to remember what was in it for the women's luncheons I serve back home. Don't you think they would like this, Kati?"

"I think it would be a big hit," Kati replied.

After a shorter than expected wait, and some polite conversation, the waiter and an assistant appeared with their dinners.

"This looks yummy," Kim said, cutting into a tender steak on the plate set before her.

The Austin Fires

"Absolutely wonderful," Clint said, spearing a small potato and placing it in his mouth.

"Really delicious," Lance agreed, "but then that's what Texas is known for. They are supposed to have the best steaks in the country."

"No question about that," Clint added.

Stormy noticed that everyone had ordered a steak dinner, except for Amy. She was busily picking at a large salad topped with pieces of chicken and covered with a light dressing.

She must be watching her weight, Stormy thought, cutting off a piece of her own steak and putting it into her mouth. *This is worth breaking any diet for in my book.*

After they finished dinner, a few of them chose desserts from the dessert cart. Kim and Kati decided to order Cherries Jubilee, which they said they'd always wanted to try.

A few minutes later, the waiter returned with two bowls of vanilla ice cream, a bottle of brandy, and a dish of cherries. He poured a little brandy over the cherries, and using a taper, lit the brandied cherries on fire. After the flames went down, he served the cherries over the cold ice cream. It was an impressive performance. They all enjoyed their desserts.

"What do you do for a living, Mr. Winters?" Frank bellowed out.

"I'm retired from the military. I used to work in finances for the Army," Lance told him.

"Ever miss it?" Frank questioned him.

"Not really," Lance answered. "It gives me more time now to watch my favorite football teams play and to tend to my roses."

S. A. Slack

"Roses?" Amy questioned, as the waiter refilled her water glass.

"Yes, Lance grows the best roses in the Phoenix area. You should see them," Stormy said, smiling at her husband. "He tends to his roses while I grow my vegetables. Besides roses, Phoenix has good weather for growing tomatoes, peppers, and squash—all kinds of vegetables, including a variety of citrus fruits. I also worked at the base as a receptionist, by the way. What about you, Mr. Thornton?"

"Call me Frank," he said. "I was 30 years on the railroad, running those engines up and down the line. What a job that was! Then they made me retire. They gave my job to some younger guy from Ohio."

"It practically killed him to have to retire," said Mrs. Thornton.

"There's nothing like the smell of diesel fuel or the sound of the whistle as she blows when rounding a curve," Frank shouted. Several of the other customers stopped their conversations to look his way.

"Speak softer, Frank," Nancy cautioned her husband, placing a hand on his arm.

"What?" Frank asked her.

"What about you, Nancy?" Stormy asked before Nancy had a chance to scold Frank any further.

"Oh, I run a little craft shop back home where we live near Atlanta," Nancy said.

"Sounds like fun," Stormy said. "I love to shop in stores like that. I'm always finding the neatest things."

"We have a lot of fun going to craft stores back in the Springs, too," Kim said.

The Austin Fires

"What about you and your sister?" Amy asked Kim. "What is your story?"

Stormy noticed Tom rolling his eyes in Amy's direction as Kati answered the question.

"We run a small business together in Colorado Springs," Kati said. "Computer graphics designs, that kind of thing. Just had our boys graduate from high school, as we said, and decided to expand our business a bit."

"That sounds cool," Amy said, her eyes lighting up.

"What about you?" Kim asked her.

"Oh, I'm a student at UCLA in Los Angeles majoring in Art," replied Amy. "I am specializing in portrait drawings, though I also love to sculpt when I can find the time."

"That sounds like fun, Amy, and what about you, Mr. Peters?" Stormy asked the young man.

"I'm a med student," Tom mumbled, stirring the ice in his tea glass.

"That's where we met, at the university," Amy said, glancing at Tom.

Tom continued to look into his glass of iced tea, as the others sat in silence.

"Well, it's getting late, and we have a lot to see tomorrow," Clint said, rising to his feet. "I think I'll turn in now. I suggest you all do the same. Have a good night everyone."

"That's a good idea," Stormy said, retrieving her walking stick from where it leaned against a near by post. "Let's go Lance. I'm tired."

They all headed back to their rooms, with the exception of Tom and Amy who went out of the hotel's front doors for some fresh air.

* * *

Lance and Stormy decided to sit for a while out on the balcony adjoining their room. It was a nice September evening. Cool, but not yet too cold to sit outside once the sun had set. They had taken the precaution of spraying mosquito repellant on themselves before going outside. This was something they had to do when they sat outside their home in Phoenix this time of year too.

After an hour or so of enjoying the city lights and some quiet conversation, Lance said he was tired and would like to turn in for the night.

"I'd like to take a bath first and read for a few minutes before going to bed," Stormy told him.

"Okay, have fun, but don't stay up too late," Lance replied, heading back into their room.

"I won't be very long," Stormy said, following behind him.

She enjoyed a nice long bath in the spacious, elegant tub and got ready for bed. As she exited the bathroom, she found Lance was under the covers and already softly snoring. She grabbed her mystery book and a few pieces of black licorice out of her purse, and settled herself in a comfortable looking chair farthest from the bed so the lamp light would not wake Lance up.

Chapter Five

Stormy awoke with a start. She found that she had been dozing in the chair for some time when her book fell from her hand into her lap.

I guess I'd better be getting to bed, she thought, as she noticed that it was well past midnight. As she rose from the chair, she heard something whack the wall outside in the hall. It sounded as if it had hit the wall not far from their door. She stopped and listened. She was sure she had heard something. The sound came again, but from further down the hall. Then she heard the distinct sound of hurried footsteps.

Stormy went to the door, quietly unlocked it, and opened it up a small crack. Seeing no one around, she opened it wider and carefully stuck her head out. Focusing her eyes to the low lighting, she peered down the long hallway just in time to see a figure dressed all in black clothing, with a dark hat pulled down low over its head, duck into the stairwell at the far end of the hall and disappear from view. There was no one else around in the dimly lit hallway, so she finally closed the door and locked it once more. Walking back to the chair she had been sitting in she retrieve her book and put it back into her purse.

Very strange, Stormy thought. *That dark figure dashing through the doorway looked similar to the figure I saw near the fire. What was someone doing up this late, sneaking around the hall? And why didn't they just use the elevator instead of the stairs. It would've been alot quicker.*

With no obvious answers to her questions, she slipped off her robe and carefully slid between the sheets to avoid waking Lance. She would try to make some sense of all this in the morning.

It was a beautiful day when they awoke the next morning. Birds were singing on the balcony outside their hotel room and the street below was a bustle of traffic and early shoppers. Stormy and Lance quickly dressed for the day and joined the others downstairs. In their hurry to be at breakfast on time with the others, Stormy decided to wait until later to tell Lance what she had heard and seen the night before.

"It's going to be a great day for our Texas museum trip," Clint informed the group at breakfast.

The tour package included a free breakfast each morning of the trip. They had chosen the hotel's smaller cafe to eat in, from which mouth-watering smells filled the nearby lobby. As the group poured over the provided menus they found that there was a wonderful array of foods to choose from, each with such a tempting description it was hard to decide upon just a single one. After finally choosing and placing their orders, Clint asked for their attention and told them a little more about the museum they would be visiting.

"Sounds like it will be a fun place to visit," Amy said, "don't you think so, Tom?"

"Yeah, it sounds alright," Tom replied, looking more cheerful this morning. His face brightened even further as a waitress placed a plate piled high with a stack of buttermilk pancakes dripping with large strawberries in a bright red sauce before him. Along side, were scrambled eggs and two large strips of crisp bacon.

"This blueberry pastry is out of this world," Stormy remarked, cutting off another bite with her fork.

"They sure know how to make a good omelet here," Lance said, following his last bite with a swig of orange juice. "Ah, that was great."

"Okay people, let's get on to the museum," the tour guide said when they had all finished their breakfast.

"I hope they have a good railroad exhibit," Frank yelled out. "It is the best thing you can see."

"We'll look for it, dear," Nancy promised, following her husband out the door.

The group climbed into the waiting van outside the hotel. Amy and Tom, in blue jeans and t-shirts, climbed into the far back seat. Stormy couldn't help notice that Tom actually continued with a more pleasant look to his face.

At least he's not scowling, Stormy thought. *Good.*

Lance, dressed in navy slacks and a red short-sleeved polo shirt, removed his black 'Retired Army' cap and climbed into the back seat with Amy and Tom, allowing Stormy to sit in the middle seat with the sisters. Today the sisters wore matching shirts of soft yellow with a smiley face on the front and a pair of black jeans, playing the part as if they were twins. Stormy had opted for a red and white sailing shirt and white cotton Capri's, with a pair of white sandals and purse to compliment the outfit. Frank, in overalls and a white dress shirt, and Nancy, dressed in casual beige and white clothes with white sneakers to match, sat in the second seat, while their guide, Clint, climbed in front next to the driver.

As they drove through the streets of Austin, they admired all of the shops and beautiful landscapes that Austin has to offer. It was a short ride, and soon they were disembarking in front of the 'Bob Bullock Texas State History Museum'. It was a large impressive granite building, and there was an air of excitement about it.

Once again, the sisters asked Stormy if she could take a picture of them. They stood outside the buildings' entrance showing the museum's sign behind them. Stormy loved photography so she had no problem snapping several good shots. She then took her cell phone out of her purse and asked if she might take a few more of the two of them for her scrapbook as well. The sisters agreed, so she snapped away.

"Thanks," Kim said, taking their camera back from Stormy and looking through the digital pictures. "These look great and will be fun to show our husbands."

"Yeah, maybe they will find the time to come along with us next time," Kati said, laughing as she looked over Kim's shoulder at the camera.

The group entered the building and were met by a young brown-haired woman in a sharp looking black skirt and white blouse. The guide had been previously

The Austin Fires

arranged by Texas' Great Tours to show them around the vast building.

"There are three floors of exhibits for visitors to see here at the museum, so I hope you have scheduled a few hours to do it justice," the guide said. "Let me start off by telling you a little about its' history. It was named after the former Texas Lt. Governor, Bob Bullock. The first floor is called 'Land', the second floor is known as 'Identity', and the third floor, 'Opportunity'. The exhibits are not 'fixed' exhibits, but are on loan and are constantly changing, so visitors will see new and interesting displays throughout the year, encouraging them to come back again and again."

"The first floor exhibits date back to the time before Texas became a state when the Native Americans first met with the Europeans," she said, ushering the group on to the exhibits.

"Look over here, Storm," Lance said, motioning with his hand for her to come over to where he was standing.

"Isn't this fascinating," Stormy said, as she stepped over to where Lance stood in front of a display of a family of American Indians canoeing down a river.

"And we have two more floors to go after this," Kati chimed in from directly behind them.

Stormy looked over her shoulder at a smiling Kati and returned her smile. Looking past her, she spotted Kim perusing a nearby display showing several more Native Americans that were sitting around a camp fire in discussion with one another.

"Hey, Kati, come look at this," Kim beckoned to her.

"I'll be right there," Kati replied. Turning back to Stormy and Lance she asked, "Do you know the Butterfields from North Phoenix, Jeff and Helen, by any chance?"

"No, I've never heard of them," Lance said. "How about you?" he asked, turning to Stormy.

"Sorry, I haven't either," Stormy replied. "Why, are they friends of yours?"

"Oh, just someone I used to know," she replied, rather quickly. "I'd better see what Kim wants." With that, she dashed off to join her sister.

"What was that all about?" Lance asked, a little bewildered at Kati's answer.

"I wonder," Stormy mused. "Well, let's get going. The tour guide is heading for the next level."

* * *

On the second floor, the 'Identity" level, they found many interesting exhibits. They saw displays of Stephen F. Austin talking from his jail cell in Mexico, and the revolution shown through the eyes of Juan Mirabeau and Sam Huston. They went from display to fascinating display, each even better than the last one.

Engrossed in a display of the 'Confederate Texas and the Civil War', Stormy realized that she hadn't been paying much attention to the others in their group. Now looking around she spotted Frank and Nancy talking with their young museum guide at the far end of the room. Nancy was rummaging in her big tapestry bag and pulled forth what looked like a statue of a black cat. She handed it over to the guide and they proceeded to look it over very carefully.

Strange things Nancy keeps in that bag of hers, Stormy thought, shaking her head as she continued to look around the room. No one else was in sight, except for her husband, Lance. Where had the others gone.

Stormy spotted a 'Restrooms' sign near a large display of soldiers that were dressed in sharp military uniforms standing at attention for what looked to be some kind of inspection. At that moment, Amy appeared through the short hallway leading from the restrooms. She seemed upset, and Stormy could see tears running down her face as she turned and walked to a nearby display and pretended interest in it. A few moments later, Tom appeared out and stood beside her. Putting his arm around her waist, he drew her in closer to him and they talked in hushed voices.

A few minutes later, Kim and Kati emerged from the restroom, laughing and carrying on. They looked like they were having a good time.

"I wonder what they found so funny in the restroom." Lanced asked.

"I don't know, but I wonder if it has something to do with the reason Amy is crying," Stormy suggested. "By the way, did you see where our 'Texas' Great Tours' guide, Clint, has gone to?" Stormy asked. "Wasn't he going to accompany us on this tour?"

"I heard him say something about checking out a place for us to have lunch," Lance said, turning from where he had just finished listening to a recording of the history of Texas.

The museum's guide approached them with the Thorntons, and the two sisters joined them.

"Okay, let's go up to the third floor and look around, then off to your lunch," she said, smiling. She led the way and the others followed close behind. Tom and Amy followed more slowly.

The third floor, or 'Opportunity' floor, showed displays of the history of oil and ranching in Texas. There were also many of the planes of the U.S. Military, from the Navy and Army Air corp.

"Look, there's the train display," Frank suddenly shouted. "Come on, Nancy." Away Frank dashed with Nancy hurrying to keep up.

"He should be happy for awhile," Lance laughed. "Let's look at the sports area over here."

Everyone has their own loves, Stormy thought, as she followed after Lance.

Chapter Six

Three quarters of an hour later, as Stormy was leaning on her walking stick in front of a display about oil tankers, she was startled to smell smoke. She looked about to see where Lance had gone. Spotting him and the sisters on the other side of the room, she proceeded to head their way. As she neared an alcove in the wall, orange and yellow flames suddenly leapt out in front of her from a metal trashcan sitting back in its recesses. Stormy jumped up against the nearby wall, startled. As the flames receded, she steadied herself with her stick and started forward once again to have a better look. The flames were spilling out onto the wall and floor around the can, and they burned more fiercely with each passing moment. Heavy black smoke billowed forth past Stormy out into the room causing her to pull a scarf from a pocket and place it tightly over her nose and mouth.

She noticed a red fire extinguisher hanging on the corner of the outside wall near the alcove on the other side of the fire. Hurriedly she dashed through the smoke to the other side and then on to the wall beyond. Slowly she inched her way along the wall to the corners' edge, continuing to cover her face with the scarf. Reaching the hanging extinguisher, she set her stick against the wall and unlatched the extinguisher's clips. Pulling it free from the clips, she aimed it at the fire and pressed down the lever sending a jet of colorful foam at the burning trash can. She continued to press the lever until all the flames were extinguished. Setting down the empty bottle and removing her scarf, Stormy wiped her hands with the scarf and sighed in relief.

Lance arrived beside her as she turned from the fire. The rest of the group was not far behind him, all except for Tom.

"What is going on, Stormy?" Lance shouted in concern. "Are you alright?"

"I'm fine, Lance," she said, as he held her tight. "I smelled smoke in the air and turned to see where you were. As I was headed across the room, the garbage can in this alcove suddenly burst into flames."

"Pretty good aim, Mrs. Winters," Tom remarked, appearing suddenly behind them from the direction she had come.

"How did this happen?" the museum guide asked, shaking her head. "I'd better call the curator and get him up here right away. He can call the fire department if he decides it is necessary to do so. I'll be right back." Rushing to a red phone on a wall across the room, she picked it up and quickly dialed a number.

Stormy stepped closer to investigate the burned out can as the others engaged in excited conversation.

"Wow! That could have burned the whole building down," Kati said, shaking her head.

"Probably some careless person tossed their cigarette in there," Kim suggested. "Some people don't care where they throw those smoldering butts."

"Maybe, but the sign downstairs says there is no smoking allowed in the museum," said Stormy, returning to stand beside Lance.

"Maybe one of the museum workers disobeyed the rules," Amy said.

"Yeah, probably so," Tom said, shoving his hands into his pockets.

Putting the phone back in its holder on the wall, the museum guide returned to the group.

"The curator has asked that you please remain here until he arrives. He would like to ask you a few questions," she said. "And thanks, Mrs. Winters for your quick actions."

"I'm glad I could be of help," Stormy replied.

"We'll be happy to wait and talk with the curator," Lance said.

"Thanks," the guide said, and headed toward the elevator to wait for the curator's arrival.

"Lance, come over here a minute," Stormy quietly said, guiding him back toward the alcove. The walls were black and the odor of smoke hung heavily upon the air.

"What do you smell? Besides the smoke, I mean?" she asked.

Lance sniffed the air and stood there in thought for a few moments.

"It smells kind of like lamp oil, or maybe kerosene," he said.

"That's exactly what I thought," she agreed. "What's this?"

Stormy bent over and picked up an object from off the floor. She held it up so that both she and Lance could examine it. In the palm of her hand she held a small silver earring in the shape of a sea horse. Inserted in its' eye was a small blue topaz. It sparkled as Stormy moved it from side to side in the overhead lights.

"I wonder how this got here," Stormy said, continuing to examine it.

"It probably fell out of someone's ear and dropped to the floor," Lance suggested, raising an eyebrow. "Maybe someone who was in a bit of a hurry."

"Maybe so," Stormy said. "I wonder who."

The sound of the elevator doors opening at the far end of the room alerted them to the arrival of the museums' curator. Knowing that they would have to turn over the earring to the curator, Stormy pressed the earring into Lance's hand. She quickly took the cell phone from her purse, opened it, and took a few pictures of the small earring Lance held. She closed the phone and slipped it back into her purse.

The curator spent the next half hour questioning the group. No, no one had seen anyone else on this level besides their group. No, none of them had been smoking, as the museum guide could verify.

Since Stormy had been nearest to the fire when it flared up, and since she was the one who had put it out, the curator questioned her more in-depth than the others. She handed over the silver and topaz sea horse earring, telling him where and how she had discovered it. After examining it, he thanked her and withdrew a clean, white

The Austin Fires

handkerchief from his pocket. He placed the earring into it, wrapped it up carefully, and placed it in the pocket of his sport coat. She, of course, made no mention of the pictures she had taken of it with her cell phone.

Finally, they were told that they could leave, but to be advised that the museum might want to question them again as the fire was investigated further.

The museum guide insisted upon escorting the group down to the ground floor level, and then excused herself at the front entrance doors.

Once outside, they were met by Clint. On hearing of their little adventure, he suggested that a nice lunch was just what they needed after such an ordeal. He ushered them to the curb where a waiting van took them to a downtown barbeque, where the smells made their mouths water even before they entered the cheerful looking café.

Over lunch, the group was abuzz with discussion over the museum fire as Clint tried to discuss the rest of the day's activities.

"I wonder how that can started on fire?" Amy asked, nibbling at a large potato wedge.

I wonder if it was an accident or if someone wanted to burn the museum down," Kim said.

"Maybe it was arson in an attempt to collect on the museum's insurance," Kati suggested.

"I guess we'll never know for sure," Clint said. "Now, as for the rest of..."

"Boy, Texas sure has some good barbeque," Kim said, interrupting him. She took a big bite of the barbequed roast beef sandwich she held between her two hands and followed it with a sip of her soda.

"These ribs are absolutely delicious," Kati agreed.

"I wonder if they ever give out their recipes." Nancy said, sopping up the last of the barbeque sauce on her plate with a bite of sandwich.

"I'll ask the waitress when she returns," said Frank, noisily slurping the last of his soda. "Maybe I can get a refill from her, too."

"After lunch," Clint said, raising his voice above the others and calling for everyone's attention, "we will have time to do a little shopping at the nearby shops, then back to the hotel for a rest before dinner. After dinner, we'll take a van out to the bridge to see the bats fly at sunset. It's quite a sight to see."

"I've been looking forward to seeing that display ever since I read the brochures on Austin," Amy said. "It sounds really exciting."

"Watch out, there might be vampires about," Tom sneered, changing his voice to fit the part. "You'd better wear your green turtle neck sweater, my dear."

"Don't worry, these are harmless bats, Mr. Peters," Clint assured them.

"That's a good thing, or we might need your services, Tom," Stormy said, laughing.

"I've got a little military training from the medics when I was in the Army that I could throw in, too," Lance suggested.

"Wasn't that a veterinarian that you served under for a while?" Stormy said, her blue eyes twinkling.

The table broke out in laughter.

They all spent the next few hours browsing the small shops along the street, each buying an item or two to take back to the hotel. With their purchases in hand, the van took them back to the Drakeston, where they went their

The Austin Fires

separate ways. The sisters headed for the massage room for their appointment with the message therapist, while Tom and Amy went to check out the swimming facilities. The Thorntons joined Lance and Stormy in the elevator heading up to their rooms.

"What a day we've had," Frank said as they stepped off the elevator on the third floor. "I think I'll lie down for awhile."

"I think I will, too," Nancy seconded. "It sounds like it's going to be a busy night."

"See you later on at dinner," Stormy said as she and Lance turned and headed for own their room.

After taking a shower and washing her hair twice, Stormy put on a fresh outfit. Glad to be out of her smoke scented clothes, she laid down on the bed. Lance took his turn at a quick shower, dressed for the evening's activities, and then opened up his laptop at the desk.

"Very strange, don't you think?" Stormy asked Lance from the bed.

"What's that?" Lance asked as he browsed through his e-mail.

"These fires," she said. "This is the second one in the two days since we arrived in Texas. I find that rather a strange coincidence, don't you?"

"Yes, now that you mention it. It does seem odd," Lance said, "but it might be just that, a coincidence."

"I wonder if that earring I found has anything to do with the fire at the museum?" she said, pulling a blanket over her cold feet and legs.

"Let me see that cell phone of yours."

"It's in my purse over there on the chair," Stormy said, pointing toward the chair by the dresser as she started to rise from the bed.

"Stay put, Storm. I'll get it."

Lance retrieved the cell phone from Stormy's purse and plugged it into his laptop with a cable he had brought with him for just this reason. With a few clicks, he had the pictures of the earring, plus the others she had taken along the trip, loaded and saved on his computer. He pulled up the pictures of the earring and displayed them on his laptop's screen.

"That sure is a pretty earring," Stormy said, coming up behind Lance and putting her hands on his shoulders. She rubbed them as she often did at home. "I'll bet whoever lost that will be looking for it. Maybe they will check with the museum's lost and found. Then they will know who dropped it."

"Not if they had anything to do with that fire, they won't" Lance said, printing off a copy of the earring on his small printer and handing it to her.

"Yes, you're right," she replied. "Thanks, I'll put this picture in my purse just in case we find the other one some where."

Lance handed her back her cell phone and she placed it back into her purse along with the photograph. Lance played a few games on his laptop while Stormy got a few winks of rest before they had to join the others down stairs for dinner.

Chapter Seven

When Stormy awoke, Lance was not quite ready to go down for dinner so she left the room and headed for the ice machine down the hallway. She would stock up with ice for later that night and put it into the small refrigerator unit in their room.

On her way back to the room, she met Amy as she stepped into the hallway from her own room. She wore a nice pair of black slacks and a pretty rose-colored blouse.

"Hello, Amy," Stormy said, balancing the bucket of ice in one hand as she made her way with the help of her walking stick in the other.

"Hi, Mrs. Winters," Amy said, smiling at her. "Here. That must be heavy. Let me help you with it."

"Thanks, and call me Stormy," she said, handing Amy the container. "Are you going down for dinner?"

"Just on my way," Amy said, carrying the ice bucket in front of her.

"Where is Tom?" Stormy asked.

"He went down a little earlier and said he would meet me in the restaurant."

"Tom doesn't seem too thrilled to be here," Stormy said, walking beside Amy down the hall.

"It's not that," she replied. "He's just worried about the new classes he'll be starting next week. He has a lot of pressure on him."

"I'll bet. College classes can be hard, especially medical classes I would think," Stormy said.

"They can be, but that's not what's bothering him so much," Amy confided. "There are a couple of things that are bothering him. First, his dad is a doctor, and he is putting a lot of pressure on Tom to be first in his class--all of his classes."

"That would be hard. It is too bad some parents never learn," Stormy said.

"I think that is why Tom's dad gave us this tour as a gift before classes start," she said. "Maybe so Tom would relax and feel better about his classes and could handle them better."

"That could be," Stormy agreed. "And what is the other thing? You mentioned a couple of things."

"Well. I probably shouldn't bring this up," she said, a worried look on her face, "but Tom's dad was involved in a malpractice suit a few months back and it has devastated Tom. One of his dad's patients died and her husband sued him, something about him misdiagnosing his wife's condition and giving her the wrong medication, or some thing like that. It was in all of the papers. His dad decided to move his practice to San Diego."

The Austin Fires

"Now that would be a tough situation to be in," Stormy sympathized with her. "I'm sorry to hear that. Maybe this trip will help him feel a little better. Well, I'd better get back before Lance misses me. I will see you down stairs in a few minutes."

"Okay, Mrs. Winters, ah Stormy," Amy said, handing the ice bucket back to her.

"Thanks, Amy, for your help."

All of the others in the party were seated around the table when Lance and Stormy arrived at the café. They placed their orders and soon were eating another delicious meal. The conversation turned toward the upcoming trip out to see the bats. They had to be there at least thirty minutes before sunset or risk missing the show. The group hurried and ate, opting to skip dessert for the time being. They piled into the van in their now usual seating arrangement and headed off for the bridge.

They made good time, arriving at the site with a few minutes to spare, and headed for the docks on the Town Lake shore. The Congress Avenue Bridge was nearby and was already filled with hundreds of spectators waiting to see the flight of the bats. There the group boarded a large tour boat and headed out into the lake for the bat watching excursion.

"This is a beautiful lake," Stormy said to Lance, "and look at those lovely trees."

"Reminds me of the lake my uncle had a cabin on up in Montana," Lance reminisced. "I spent a summer there once with my cousins. Boy, were they ever a wild bunch."

"Oh, look!" Kati exclaimed. "The bats are coming."

Lance and Stormy turned their attention skyward.

S. A. Slack

First, they saw one bat, and then another and another until the whole sky was filled with the bats. As they flew closer to the boat, they could see that the bats were only about half the size of a human hand.

"I've never seen so many bats in one place before," Frank shouted.

The sky above the boat was filled with a dark cloud of the winged creatures. Loud peeping noises came from the bats as they flew by.

"Wow! Have you ever seen such a sight?" Kim said, craning her neck to get a better view.

There must be over a million bats up above us," Amy guessed.

"Probably closer to two million," Lance suggested, scanning the sky. "It's a pretty sight indeed."

They all watched the show in amazement as the bats continued to fly over them. The bats circled around the lake and under the nearby bridge. They landed in the trees, and then took off again, circling the area repeatedly.

"Yuck," Stormy said, looking at the boats rim next to her. "I thought that only birds dropped poop from the air."

"Well, I guess when they have to go they don't have time to look for a rest area," Lance said, grinning.

"Oh, Lance" she said, socking him on the arm. "Just wait until they get you."

As the sun finished setting and the sky turned black, the boats' crew turned on a huge red light and shined it at the bats. The group could see the bats much more clearly as they continued their flight over the lake and along its' banks.

The Austin Fires

They continued to watch the aerial show above, when suddenly a large splash sounded from the direction of the boat's stern. Stormy turned toward the noise and saw that several people were leaning over the edge of the boat and peering down into the water.

"Help, woman over board," an older man yelled. "Get some help over here right away."

Stormy stood up and started for the rear of the boat, followed closely by Lance. By the time they arrived, two crew members were pulling a woman out of the water with the help of a long pole which had a rope attached to its end. As they brought her on board, Stormy was startled to see that the dripping wet woman was Amy.

"My goodness, what happened?" Stormy said, pushing her way through the crowd. "Are you all right?"

"The water is freezing cold," Amy said, shivering.

One of the crewmembers brought her a large blanket, wrapping it around her shoulders.

"I came to the back of the boat to get a better view of the bats in the trees on shore over there," she said, wringing out her dripping wet hair. "I was looking through a small pair off binoculars I had brought with me, when someone ran by me, knocking me over the edge of the boat and into the water below."

"Do you think they did it on purpose?" Stormy asked, handing Amy an extra towel to dry her hair with from the pile near where she stood.

"I don't know. It was probably just an accident," Amy replied, as Tom came to her side.

"In for a swim, Amy?" Tom chuckled. "Good thing you know how to swim." He sat down beside her on the bench, and taking the towel from out of her hands, began rubbing down her wet hair.

Stormy excused herself and turning around, walked back to where Lance was standing looking on. She took him to one side so as not to be overheard.

"What was that all about?" he asked her. "Is Amy alright?"

"Yes, it looks like she will be just fine," Stormy replied, then repeated what Amy had told her. "I wonder though, if it really was just an accident, or if some one pushed her in on purpose?"

"I wonder what reason they would have for that?" he said.

"Who knows, but too many things have happened to be just coincidence," she said.

Stormy went on to tell Lance about the shadowy figure she had spotted near the bus fire the previous day. She also told him about the noises she heard outside their room in the hall late last night, and about the darkly dressed figure she saw dashing through the stairwell door.

"The next time you see or hear something out of the ordinary, let me know about it, will you? I'll check it out with you," said Lance. "It isn't good for you to go it alone with all that's been happening here."

"Okay," she agreed.

As Lance looked back in Amy's direction, Stormy overheard two women talking together on the bench behind her.

"Did you hear what happened at the back of the boat, Joan?" the one woman said.

The Austin Fires

"I heard a big splash and then some kind of commotion about a woman falling in the lake," said the other woman. "Why, what happened, Sarah?"

"They say that someone came up from behind this woman and purposely pushed her into the water," Sarah said. "It sounds like someone was trying to do away with her, if you ask me."

"It could be," Joan replied. "I have read about such things before. They say it's a good way to get rid of someone and make it look like an accident."

"Who says that?"

"I read it in one of those papers at the grocery store checkout."

They might be more right than they know, Stormy thought.

Amy insisted that she was fine and that they should continue with the bat tour as planned. There were no more mishaps and everyone enjoyed the remainder of the show.

Afterwards, the boat docked back at the shore and the group took the van back to the hotel. It was getting late as Lance and Stormy headed to their room. The two sisters headed for the café on the main floor, saying that they wanted to get some ice cream before retiring. Frank and Nancy decided to join them. As for Amy, she thought it would be best to take a nice long bath and change into warm pajamas. Tom agreed that would be best. He wanted to get some fresh air and told her he wouldn't be long.

Stormy and Lance once again enjoyed sitting outside on their balcony before they retired for the night. They talked over the events of their trip so far, and they wondered what was going on and if these things would continue to happen. They hoped it would not ruin the entire trip.

"On our next trip, I think we might forget the tour idea and go it alone," Lance said, as he sipped his diet soda.

"Maybe that would be a good idea," she agreed. "I hope we're not in the middle of some murder mystery here."

"I hope not, too," he said. "I think you should read less of those murder mysteries and read some of my science fiction books. You might find them a little less gruesome."

"Yeah, right," she said, making a face at him.

"Well, let's call it a night and get to bed," he said, laughing.

Standing up from the lounge chair, Stormy looked out at the lights of the city.

"Austin sure is a lovely place," she said.

As she turned to go inside, a movement on the street below caught her eye. Across the street, standing on the sidewalk in the glow of a streetlight, she saw a man who looked a lot like Tom. On closer look, she saw that it was Tom. He was talking to a man whose back was turned to her. As she watched, she saw Tom hand the man something in an envelope which the man shoved deep into his pocket. They continued in quiet conversation for a few more minutes, and then the man left. Tom crossed the street and headed for the hotel.

Lance had already stepped back into their room, and Stormy quickly went inside, closed the balcony doors, and drew the drapes over them.

The Austin Fires

"I saw Tom across the street talking to a man," she told Lance. "He handed the man something in an envelope. I wonder what he's up to.

"Maybe the man just wanted directions to some place, and Tom wrote them down for him," Lance said.

"I guess," she said, deep in thought, "but why put it into an envelope?"

"Maybe so he wouldn't misplace it. Come on. Let's get some sleep," he said, pulling her onto the bed.

Chapter Eight

In the morning, the sky was overcast with a few dark clouds. They all enjoyed another wonderful breakfast of pancakes and eggs before heading out for the day. Piling in the van, they headed north to the grounds of the University of Texas at Austin.

"First, we will spend the morning with a tour of the U of T's campus. I hope you all wore good walking shoes like I suggested last night. Then we'll have a little lunch before heading back to the hotel. You are on your own then until after dinner," Clint said, speaking loudly from the front seat of the van so all could hear him. "Then, of course, we'll attend the Longhorn's football game this evening."

"That will be great!" Lance said from the back seat, obviously excited at the prospect.

"Yeah," Frank loudly chimed in.

They arrived at the University of Texas at Austin's 357-acre campus, and made their way to the tours' office.

Once there, they were given maps of the area and were told that the walking tour, called 'Walking the Forty Acres', would encompass the original forty acres that were set aside by the founding fathers for higher education.

Armed with maps and various reading materials, the group headed out. The papers they were handed talked of the areas various types of limestone and granite, which most of the buildings were made of. These were some of the original buildings of the university.

Their first stop was the 'Biology Building' and 'Painter Hall'. Here they saw that the buildings were made of granite and Cordova Limestone.

"The limestone was quarried right here in Austin," Clint said, "and as you will see later on, it is even used in many of the homes and buildings around Austin today."

They saw beautiful red marble placed above the north entrance of one of the buildings they were walking by. Stormy thought that it would look great in the entrance of their home in Phoenix.

The next stop was labeled 'Welch Hall'. It, too, was built of the same limestone, but with a base, door sills, and steps made of Pearl Granite.

On they proceeded, building after building. The group marveled at the designs of each new building they came to, done in limestone and accented by various colors of granite and marble. The Vermont Blue and Purple Slate were outstanding at Calhoun Hall, as was the Pink Granite at Battle Hall.

As they neared Goldsmith Hall, Stormy's feet were hurting, and she had a cramp in her left leg. Spotting a bench up ahead, she told Lance that she had to sit down and rest for a few minutes. The group went on to see the

The Austin Fires

next building, leaving Lance and Stormy to sit on the bench.

After a short while, and some leg rubbing from Lance, Stormy was feeling much better. They arose, left the bench, and headed towards the next stop on the route, 'Hog Auditorium'.

As the auditorium came into view, they saw some of their group up ahead of them in front of the building in a discussion of the buildings limestone. They spotted Nancy standing near the street holding her large tapestry bag and looking into the deep reaches of it in search of who knows what.

They were about to hail her when a person with a dark jacket on and a ski mask pulled low over their face, leapt out of the nearby bushes, knocked her down, and ran off with her bag. The figure then proceeded to dash across the road and disappeared behind another building. It happened so fast that neither of them had time to react before the thief was gone from sight.

Stormy dashed ahead with Lance close on her heels. As they arrived at the spot where Nancy had fallen, they saw that Frank, too, had seen what happened and was on his way. He covered the space quickly between them and the building he had been standing in front of with the rest of the group. Stormy was surprised to see that he could move so fast when the need arose.

"Nancy, are you alright my dear?" Frank shouted, as he reached her. She had sat up and was gingerly rubbing her ankle.

"Did you injure your ankle?" Stormy asked.

"Probably so. It really hurts something terrible," she replied, moaning. "But more important, Frank, they took my bag. I've got to get it back."

"Don't worry, we will," he assured her.

The tour group had gathered around Nancy. They were all concerned for her and wanted to know how they could help. Clint ran off to the office to get some assistance.

"Let me take a look at that ankle, Mrs. Thornton," Tom said, squatting down next to her, "if that would be alright with you, of course."

"Okay, please do," Nancy replied, her face twisted in pain as she held onto her ankle.

Tom checked her out with the skilled hands of a trained medical professional, taking care not to cause any further pain.

"It doesn't appear to be broken. Probably just a twisted ligament, but it wouldn't hurt to have an x-ray of it just in case," he said. Just then Clint and the man from the university they had talked to earlier came hurrying up.

"What is going on around here?" Frank demanded of Clint, in a loud angry tone of voice. "First, we have two fires that could have injured any one of us, then the young woman there gets pushed over board into the lake, and now someone knocks down my wife, steals her purse, and hurts her ankle." Red in the face with rage, he continued, "We came on this tour to relax and have a good time. We are not having a very good time, and I am not sure it is safe to continue on any further with your tour."

"Calm down, Mr. Thornton," Clint soothed the angry man. "I'm sorry about your wife, but it is just a few unfortunate incidents that could have happened to any

The Austin Fires

one, though we have never had such bad luck as this on any of our other tours. I can assure you that you and your wife will be perfectly safe continuing on the rest of the tour with us. You all will be."

"We will see," Frank said, looking a little calmer as he held onto Nancy's hand.

"Let's take her inside and get her out of the sun," the University man interjected into the conversation. "The campus police are on their way."

Tom offered to carry Nancy to the office with Frank's help. They made a chair by linking their crossed arms together, and lifted her as carefully as they could. Off they went at a slow pace to avoid further injury. The police soon arrived, followed by an ambulance. As the paramedics examined Mrs. Thornton, the police officers questioned the group. Stormy and Lance told them what they had seen. Along with the description from Nancy, herself, and Frank, the police started a thorough search throughout the area.

"It would help more if we had a description of the perpetrators face, but we'll see what we can do," one of the officers said.

The police continued to scour the scene for any clues as the paramedics put Nancy into the awaiting ambulance. They agreed with Tom that she'd probably just twisted her ankle but should have it x-rayed to make sure there wasn't a hairline fracture. Frank got into the back of the vehicle with his wife and off they went to the hospital.

"Never a dull moment with this group," Lance said, watching the ambulance disappear down the street.

"That's for sure," Stormy replied. "I wonder if that person had been following us, waiting for the chance that

Nancy might be alone for a moment. I hope they find that bag of hers. She seems very attached to it."

"Did that figure look like a man to you, Stormy?" Lance asked her.

"It did to me, but since we could not see their face or much of their body, it was hard to tell. I hope the police will find someone that saw a bit more of the thief's appearance than we did."

"Let's all get in the van and head for lunch. They have some great places here on the campus," Clint said. "I think you'll enjoy the food. And don't worry, the hospital will take good care of the Thorntons."

After a great lunch of delicious roast beef sandwiches, onion potato chips, and cole slaw, they got back on the road.

"Before we go back to the hotel, I want to stop one more place," Clint said, smiling. "It is one of my favorite places to visit each time I come to Austin. I think you'll like it, too."

The van took them to the town of Round Rock and pulled upto a small shop beneath a tall water tower which bore the name of the town across its side. The sign above the shop read 'Bakery' and the smell that came from its ovens was heavenly as they entered the shop. They looked at a display of doughnuts, cakes, breads, pies, and cookies laid out in front of them. There were sausages wrapped in bread and big blueberry muffins.

"Ooh, look at these doughnuts," Kim said, eyeing a large crème filled one.

"They look wonderful," Kati said. "They're not on my diet, but maybe one won't hurt me."

The Austin Fires

"I'll take a dozen of these doughnuts," Clint said to the sales woman behind the desk. "Let me have three of those and another three of those beside them. I'll have two of those jelly ones, and four of the chocolate crèmes, please."

"Look at the color of the dough, Lance," Stormy said, pointing at one of the cake like doughnuts in the case in front of her. "It's an orange color and quite heavy from the looks of it."

"That's what makes them taste so good," the woman behind the counter said, offering them a sample to try.

"This tastes great," Lance said, wiping a crumb from off his lip. "Let's get a few extras to take back to the hotel, Storm."

"I agree," Stormy replied, choosing a few from the many choices behind the glass.

After they had all bought some delicious looking items, they climbed into the van and headed for the hotel.

Back at the Drakeston, they separated and went off on their own for the rest of the afternoon. The sisters declared that they wanted to do more shopping after they freshened up in their room. Amy and Tom decided to stroll down Sixth St. and look in on some small shops and pubs in the area. Stormy and Lance decided to rest and read for awhile, then they would decide what they would do for the rest of the afternoon. Frank and Nancy had not yet returned from the emergency room at the hospital.

When they reached their room, Lance opened his laptop and turning it on, proceeded to check his e-mail. Stormy sat on the bed and took a small notebook and pencil from her purse. Tossing the purse on a nearby chair, she leaned back against the headboard and flipped the notebook open. She began scribbling away, stopping to ponder and then writing some more.

"What are you doing?" Lance asked, turning from his computer.

"Making a list," she answered, keeping her eyes on the page where she had just written something down.

"A list of what?" he said, showing more interest.

"Of all the strange things that have happened to our tour group since we left the Dallas/Ft.Worth airport a few days ago," she said. "I'm writing down all the names of the members of our group, as well."

"Ah, and you expect to learn something from these lists?" Lance asked, raising a questioning eyebrow.

"Well, something strange is going on here," she said. "I don't think this is all just coincidence any more. Too many things have taken place in such a short time. This is not normal."

"How would you know? Maybe it is for these people," said Lance, grinning.

"Maybe, but somehow I doubt it," she replied, scribbling another few lines down in her notebook.

"Okay, what do you have so far?" Lance asked, opening a window on his laptop and preparing to type.

"First, I have written down all the names of everyone in our group and left a large space underneath each one of them. This will give me room to write down their ages, where they have come from, their occupations, things I've noticed about them, et cetera." Stormy said.

"Sounds good so far," he said, his fingers flying over the computer's keys.

"What are you doing?" Stormy asked, looking up from her notebook.

The Austin Fires

"I thought it would be easier to put your notes in the computer," he said, typing a few more lines. "You can transfer the notes from your notebook there each chance you get and see the over all picture better on here."

"Thanks, Lance," she replied, knowing how he loved to help her out whenever he could, not to mention using his computer in any way he could. "That is very thoughtful of you."

"Then on to your next page," he said, fingers at the ready.

"I'm making a list of what has happened so far and who was involved in it, as far as we know. Also, I have a column for any items we have found, or what we have observed about those incidences," she related. "Also, how things might be connected together."

"Sounds like a pretty thorough list," Lance said, typing away. "You'll be a Sherlock Holmes in no time."

"Thanks, and you can be my Watson," she said, throwing a pillow in his direction.

Stormy continued working on her notebook, scratching out words here and there, and tearing out a page. She tossed it aside and started over again on a fresh piece while Lance perfected his program to hold all of her information and process it better.

"Here's a new pencil, Storm," Lance said, tossing her one from the bunch he always carried in his laptop case. "It'll help save your fingers from that stub you're working with."

"That would help," she replied, picking up the pencil from off the pillow near her head.

They both worked in silence for a while and then Stormy read off a few more items for Lance to punch into his computer list.

"I think we had better call it quits for now," Lance said, looking at his watch. "It's time to join the others for dinner."

Instead of eating in the hotels' restaurant, they would meet outside of the hotel and head to a hamburger place, then on to the game.

Frank and Nancy had finally returned from the hospital and Lance and Stormy checked in on them before going downstairs. Frank said that the doctors had x-rayed Nancy's ankle and found that it was not broken. However, they found that she had torn ligaments from the fall and advised her to stay off it for a few days, giving her a pair of crutches to use. Frank said he would forgo the game and stay with Nancy at the hotel. He could always watch it later on video, anyway.

"Do you want us to bring you back some burgers before we head out to the game?" Stormy asked them.

"No thanks, we will order something from the hotel's café and have it sent up to us," Frank replied in a softer voice than usual.

"Okay, see you later," Lance said, turning to leave.

They wished Nancy a speedy recovery and left the room to join the others for dinner.

Chapter Nine

Stormy found the hamburgers delicious and especially enjoyed the large chocolate crème milk shake accompanying it. When they had finished eating, they piled back into the van and headed for the Darrell K. Royal-Texas Memorial Stadium. They were all excited about the game. The Texas Longhorns were playing the Oklahoma State Cowboys tonight.

"It should be quite a game tonight," Lance said, excited over the prospect.

"Yes, and we were able to get you some pretty good seats, so I'm sure you will enjoy the game even more," Clint said, turning in his seat.

The parking areas were filling up quickly when they arrived at the stadium. Stormy appreciated the fact that they were dropped off at the gate and did not have to find a place to park. Clint handed them their tickets and they entered the stadium.

As they made their way to their seats down in front on the fifty-yard line, several vendors selling popcorn, peanuts, hotdogs, burgers, team hats and banners accosted them. Each purchased a hat or banner and a snack from the vendors.

"These are great seats," Lance said, placing the burnt-orange ball cap with 'Texas Longhorns' written in white letters across the front, on his head.

"We'll have a pretty good view of the game from here," Tom said, sitting down next to Amy and handing her a bag of popcorn.

Down below them, the Longhorn cheerleaders were going through their paces, shouting and waving their pom-poms to the beat as the band played. On the other side of the stadium, the Cowboys' cheerleaders were doing the same for their teams' fans. The crowd cheered and yelled through out the stadium as the cheerleaders, dressed in orange and white, from both sides jumped and flipped their way through their routines.

"What an orange filled stadium," Stormy commented, surveying the crowd.

"With both teams' colors being orange and white, you can't help but have that," Lance replied. "As you can see, most of the fans are wearing matching sweatshirts from their school's teams. That's why I'm glad we brought these orange shirts for the game."

"Yes, we do look rather good in these," she said, laughing, "even though orange is not my favorite color."

"Will you take a picture of the two of us?" Kim asked Lance, who was sitting on the other side of her.

"I sure will," he replied, taking the camera from her.

The Austin Fires

Kim and Kati posed together holding burnt-orange and white banners. They stood with their backs to the field while Lance took several shots of them. Then he took a small digital camera of his own out of his pocket and took a few shots of the whole group and a couple of the field and fans. He would take more of the actual players themselves during the game.

"Lance, do you think you could get individual photos of each of the members in our group?" Stormy asked him quietly.

"Sure, I think I can arrange that," he said, lowering his voice. "Why alone?"

"It's for the lists I am compiling," she said. "If it's alright with you, I would like to transfer the rest of my notes onto your laptop and add the pictures to each person's information."

"Ah, suspects Sherlock," Lance said, chuckling. "I think ole Watson can help you out."

"It will help out a lot," Stormy said. "You know how I like to organize things."

"Yes, I noticed how my sock drawer at home had been rearranged last week," Lance teased.

"Interesting, since all of your socks are navy blue," she replied, smiling.

The game began with Oklahoma winning the coin toss for the kick-off. It was an exciting game as they watched the players running down the field. These were hard playing teams. The Texas Longhorns played in their burnt-orange jerseys, with the Oklahoma Cowboys in white ones.

As the game played out, Stormy looked around the stands. She noticed several fans near by that wore paint in the color of the Longhorns team on each of their faces. She spotted another man just behind them who had taken his shirt off. He had painted not only his face, but his whole chest and stomach in orange and white. His belly bounced up and down as he cheered for the team.

Now that's going a little over board, thought Stormy. *What fans won't do for attention.*

"Go, go, go!" Lance was yelling, standing on his feet, bringing Stormy's attention back on the field.

"Touch down by McCoy for Texas," the game announcer shouted over the loud speaker. The crowd went wild with cheers and shouting as the Longhorn band played.

During the half time show, Stormy went with Kim and Katie in search of the women's restroom. They waded through the heavy crowd, being tossed about like small boats on a river in the middle of a violent storm, pushed this way and that in their attempt to reach their destination. Once there, they stood in line for a good ten minutes. Stormy was frustrated further by the timing of the infrared toilet in the stall she occupied. Each time she would place a paper seat cover over the toilet seat it would be flushed down by the sensor before she could sit down. Finally, determined to win out over the blasted thing, she first started to sit down and then quickly slipped in the paper cover at the last minute.

"Touchdown!" Stormy quietly said to the stall around her.

Afterwards, the trio slowly made their way back toward their seats. On the way there, Stormy noticed that a man dressed in an orange Texas Longhorn shirt and blue jeans seemed to be keeping pace with them. When

The Austin Fires

the crowd stopped in front of Stormy and the sisters for a few moments, she noticed that even though the crowd was freely moving in front of the man, he too stopped and stood still, looking through his pockets in search of some unknown item. When the crowd in front of Stormy started to move once more, so did he. He continued to shadow them in this manner until they neared their seats.

Upon arriving, Stormy looked around to see where the man was, but he had disappeared from view.

"The second half is about to get under way," Lance told her. "There's quite a crowd here."

"Yes, and one in the women's restroom, too," she said. "Lance, a man was following us as we headed back to our seats."

"Maybe he's sitting in a seat close by us," said Lance.

"No, this was more than that," she assured him. "When we stopped in the crowd, so did he, even though he had a clear path in front of him. He did this several times."

"Did he follow you all the way to your seat?" Lance said, turning and looking around about them.

"Pretty close to it," she answered. "When we reached the seats, I turned and looked for him, but couldn't see him any where."

"Well, if you see him again, point him out for me. I'll see if I can catch up to him."

"Okay," Stormy said, looking around once more.

The excitement rose up around them as the game continued. Both teams made some pretty good moves, and Stormy found it interesting to watch their plays. She even felt like cheering for Oklahoma's quarter back, Reid, as he ran the field for a touch down for the Cowboys. She bit her tongue in time, and quietly enjoyed the play. After all, she was sitting on the Longhorn's side of the stadium.

Their whole group was on their feet cheering with the rest of the crowd as McCoy made a last minute touch down, winning the game for the Longhorns at 20-10. A few players from the winning team grabbed the large cooler of ice-cold sports drink and poured it over their coach's head.

"I'll bet that's cold," Amy said, laughing as the team's coach shivered and was handed a large white towel.

"Yeah, I'd think so" Kim chimed in.

"That was some game," Tom said, more animated than they had seen him act since they had met him a few days ago. Obviously, he had enjoyed the game.

"Great game," said Clint, "but we had better get going. The van will be waiting for us outside, and I'd like to beat as much of this crowd as possible out of the lot."

They turned and followed Clint toward the exit. As they were approaching the gate, Stormy spotted the man that had been following them earlier from the restrooms.

"Look, there he is. The same man that was following us," Stormy told Lance, pointing toward the gate ahead of them. "That man just going through the gate behind that red-headed woman."

Lance dashed ahead of her through the gate in an attempt to catch up to the man. He returned a few minutes later to where the others were waiting in the van. Stormy had told them that her husband had spotted an old friend and wanted to say hi.

The Austin Fires

"Sorry, Storm, he got lost in the crowd," Lance quickly told her as he climbed into the van and took his seat.

"Thanks for trying anyway."

As they were heading for the exit to the stadium parking lot, the group's van was delayed in the sudden standstill in the traffic as several fire trucks and a police car roared into the lot in front of them. The vehicles headed toward several parked cars on the far side of the lot. Not far from the cars, the group could see that flames were shooting out of an older looking vehicle's trunk into the air.

"Those tailgaters occasionally forget to put out the barbeques they cook on before they go into the stadium for the game," Clint said as the group watched the firefighters remove their hoses from the trucks to extinguish the flames.

"It's a hot time in the old Austin tonight," Tom said, as they drove out of the stadium.

As they headed back to the hotel, Stormy once again wondered what was going on. Why was some one setting fires and pushing Amy over the stern of the boat? Who knocked Nancy down, injuring her ankle and stealing her purse? Who was that sneaking around the halls late at night, and who was shadowing them at the game?

Before anyone gets more seriously hurt, or even killed, we'd better find out who is doing this, and how to make them stop, she thought.

It was late at night when they arrived back at the hotel. They said their good nights to one another and went to their rooms. Stormy wanted to find out how Nancy Thornton was doing, but due to the late hour she decided to wait until the morning to check on her.

Chapter Ten

Stormy slept soundly throughout the night and awoke feeling rejuvenated. She was just emerging from the bathroom after a nice hot shower when Lance informed her that the sky was filled with dark, forbidding clouds.

"If it rains, we may have a change of plans today," Stormy said, drying the ends of her hair with a soft yellow bath towel.

"Well, in that case I'm sure we can find something else to do instead," Lance said, grinning.

When they arrived downstairs at the café for breakfast, they found Kim and Kati enjoying omelets, hash browns, and orange juice. They were the only ones to have arrived from the group so far. Stormy and Lance sat down at the table and scanned the menus. When the waitress came back, Stormy ordered a Spanish omelet, with sausage and juice. Lance opted for a large stack of pancakes with maple syrup, eggs over easy with bacon, and a large glass of grapefruit juice.

"So how are the two of you doing this morning?" Stormy asked the sisters as they waited for their food to arrive.

"I'm fine, but Kim has a bad headache she has been trying to get rid of," Kati said, looking over at her sister. "It may slow us down a little today."

"I'll be okay as soon as this allergy medicine kicks in," Kim said. "It says it is 'Non-Drowsy', but everything makes me tired these days."

"I know what you mean. Many of the non-drowsy ones do that to me, also," Stormy said. "I think they should call it 'might not make you drowsy' medication on the label."

Tom and Amy entered the café just as the waitress brought the Winter's orders to their table.

"Good morning," Stormy said. "Did you sleep well?"

"Not really," Amy said, stifling a yawn. "It sounded like there was a party going on outside all night down in the street."

"Well, Sixth Street has a lot of music and dance clubs along it. Maybe they had their music up extra loud," Lance chimed in.

"Tonight you can visit a dance club, if you wish to," Clint said, joining them at a nearby table. "I think you will all enjoy it. They have some lively music and great bands here in Austin."

"Sounds like a lot of fun," Stormy said. "It's been a while since Lance and I have gone dancing, but I think we can still remember how."

The Austin Fires

"Why yes, my dear," Lance said, "I think we can still cut a rug or two at our age. If my knee holds out, that is."

"Speaking of dancing, how is Nancy's ankle doing this morning?" Stormy asked.

"I'm much better," Nancy said, slowly making her way to the tables, a crutch under each arm.

"They say with a few days off her foot, she'll be as good as new," Frank said, rather loudly as he pulled a chair out for his wife. "I'd love to get my hands on that scoundrel. I'd have a word or two for him. He'd never bother anyone ever again."

The look in Frank's eyes betrayed his anger. Stormy had thought him a mild man of peace, but now she was not sure what he'd do if he caught up with the person who knocked Nancy down, and she was not sure she wanted to know. Maybe it would be better if the police caught up with the perpetrator before Frank did.

As they ate their food, Clint told them about their day ahead.

"Even though it looks like we might have rain today, we'll go ahead as planned and see how the day develops. This morning we tour more of the city of Austin and the surrounding areas, and see some of its many interesting sights. Later we'll stop at Mount Bonnel and climb the 99 steps there. What a beautiful view!" he said. "I'm sorry, Mrs. Thornton, about your ankle. The things we'll be doing today will be a little hard for you to participate in."

"Oh, I will be okay," Nancy said. "I can come along for the ride and just sit in the van, or inside a near by café or store while you all tour things. I will enjoy getting out, and I don't want Frank to miss a thing."

"Only if you feel well enough, dear," Frank said, giving his wife a look of concern.

"Okay, then let's get to the van and head out to see Austin," Clint ordered the group.

They all piled into the van and were soon heading down Hwy I-35. The day was overcast, but the views were beautiful as they drove around the area. The weather had cooled down a bit, making for a more pleasant drive.

They passed streets with impressive names like Elkhorn Mt., Pecan Park Blvd., and Hunters Chase Dr. There were beautiful trees everywhere they looked, surrounded by lots of velvety green grass and colorful flowers of all types.

"What an absolutely beautiful place Austin is," Stormy remarked, "so much greener than Phoenix. We'll have to come back here again some time."

"That would be fun, but in defense of Phoenix it has greenery and flowers of its own, you know. Just look at my rose garden," Lance said. "And I really love the smell of the orange blossoms as we pass by the large orange tree groves out in Mesa."

"Yes, you're right. They are quite lovely indeed," she said.

"Look at the name of that street," Kim interrupted, pointing out the window nearest her. "It's called 'Beartrap', and that one over there is Deer Falls Dr. I'd love to live on that one."

"We should suggest some of these names for that new subdivision that your brother-in-law is helping put up in the Springs," Kati said.

The Austin Fires

"Let's do that when we get home," she replied. "Have you got a pen I could borrow? I've got my little tablet right here, but I must have dropped my pen some where."

"You know how purses are," Nancy chimed in. "I'm always losing things in the deep reaches of the pockets."

"That reminds me, Nancy," Stormy said, "did they ever recover your purse?"

"Not yet," Nancy replied. "They said they would call me if they found it, but that they held out little hope of that."

"I'm sorry to hear that," Stormy said. "You must have lost a lot of your things with it."

"Yes, you don't know the half of it," Nancy said, a note of sadness in her voice.

"Look!" Amy shouted from the back seat. "There is Scotland Yard."

"Here in Austin?" Nancy said, looking out the window. "Where do you see that?"

"And there's Parliament Place over there," Tom said, getting into the fun of it all.

"Okay, you two," Nancy said, laughing as she realized what they had meant.

The group had fun shouting out the various names as they went through a few more of the neighborhoods through out Austin. They admired the many homes and buildings made of the limestone that the area was known for.

"We should see about building a house out of this limestone back home," Frank said. "I wonder if we can get it in Georgia."

"They probably would be able to ship it there," Lance replied.

They stopped at a few stores along the way, looking at the delicious green chilies from Hatch, New Mexico. They found that several varieties were available here. Stormy was disappointed when she heard, from one of the storeowners, that they had missed the Chile festival held in Austin a few weeks earlier.

"Is any one hungry?" Clint asked as it neared noon time.

"Yes," the group chimed in together.

"There's a little hamburger and hotdog place that I think you will like not far from here," Clint told them. "It's not a very fancy place, but it has good food."

"I hope they have chicken, too," Amy said. "I've eaten too much beef on this trip."

"You'll be okay," Tom chided her.

Chapter Eleven

They stopped at a small burger place not far from the intersection of the highway they were traveling along and a cross road. Clint had been right. The building was very small, with only a few tables crowded into the eating area. The food smelled pretty good and after they ordered, they had their food in a short time.

"You're right, Clint," Frank said loudly, causing others ordering food to look his way. He wiped the catsup off his face with a napkin. "This is pretty darn good for being such a small place."

"I discovered it on a previous trip and have stopped here whenever I'm in town," Clint said, taking a big bite of his burger.

As they were finishing up, a cook came rushing from the door leading to the small kitchen in the back. He looked panicky and spoke very quickly in a foreign language. He was hard to understand, and it wasn't until black smoke poured out from the kitchen that they realized the danger and what he was shouting about.

"Everyone outside, now," the young boy behind the counter yelled, as he ran for the door. "The kitchen's on fire."

The group grabbed their things and jumped to their feet. The thickening smoke pouring from the kitchen made it hard to see, but they all managed to get outside. Tom and Lance carried Nancy out of the burning building, with Amy bringing her crutch along behind them. Their eyes burned and several in the group were coughing and sneezing as fire trucks roared up to the building.

Stormy noticed that the two sisters stood off to one side away from the group and seemed to be arguing about something. Kim was pointing back at the building while Kati was shaking her head as if to respond in the negative. This went on for a several minutes until Kati turned and stomped off in an angry huff. Stormy saw Kim shake her head as she watched her sister leave.

I wonder what those two were arguing about, Stormy mused. *Was it something about the fire?*

It took the firefighters a while to extinguish the fire and make sure all of the embers were out so it would not flare up again after they left. The Fire Chief and a police inspector were sifting through the ashes inside the burnt out shell of the building for clues as to how the fire had started. Other police were questioning both the employees and the customers. One of the firefighters approached the tour group. He asked them if he could have a few minutes of their time, which they readily agreed to.

"I'm Captain Jack Smith of the Austin Fire Dept. You may not remember me, but I was on one of the trucks that

The Austin Fires

responded to the bus fire you were involved in earlier this week," he started out. "I also heard that a group from Texas' Great Tours was at the State History Museum when a small fire burst out on the third floor there. Was that your group?"

"Yes Sir, we were there at the time of the fire," Lance answered.

"I hear that one of you women put that fire out," he said. "Which one of you did that?"

"That was my wife," Lance said, motioning to Stormy.

"You did a great job," he said. "The whole place might have gone up in flames if you had not acted so quickly."

"Thanks, Captain Smith," Stormy said.

"Now I find that you are all here at this hamburger stand when it, too, caught on fire. It seems that fire is following your group around," the Captain said. "Any ideas why?"

"No ideas, Captain Smith," Frank shouted at him. "I guess we're just unlucky to be in the wrong places at the wrong times."

"Seems that way, doesn't it," the captain mused. "Where is your group staying?"

"We're at the Drakeston Hotel, Captain," Clint offered.

"Are you going to be in the city for a while longer?" he asked Clint.

"Yes, we'll be here until the end of the week," Clint answered.

"Okay, I'll be in touch. You can go now," Captain Smith said. He turned and walked back toward the ashes.

"Well, if everyone is okay, we'll go on to our next stop now," Clint said to the group.

They all agreed to continue the tour, the sooner the better the sisters agreed.

They got back into the van and headed for their next stop. They were going to visit Mount Bonnell Park and climb its ninety-nine steps.

"This is getting quite serious," Stormy whispered to Lance as the others talked amongst themselves. "I think the Captain is right to wonder about it."

"Yes, I agree with you," Lance said, "but I wonder what we can do about it."

"I don't know yet, but let's keep our eyes and ears open and see if we can learn anything that might be of help in piecing this together."

They arrived at their destination, and the group disembarked. Nancy found a wooden bench under a nearby tree and decided she would wait there for the group. Frank wanted to stay behind with her, but Nancy urged him to at least "go and take a look". There were a few other older women sitting on the nearby benches, so she felt comfortable waiting there, she told him.

"Besides, I have my umbrella to fend anyone off, if need be," Nancy said, grinning. "You can tell me all about the view from up there when you return."

The group headed up the steps, with Amy and Tom taking the lead. The sisters followed behind them, and Lance and Stormy headed up next. Frank and Clint followed at the rear of the group.

"This is a lovely place," Stormy said to Lance.

The Austin Fires

"Yes, it is," he replied, surveying the sky. "I hope those clouds hold back the rain until we get down from here."

"I hope so, too," she replied.

It turned out to be quite a climb for the group, but when they reached the top they all agreed it was worth it. They could see far out over the city and the beautiful blue of Lake Austin below.

"Absolutely gorgeous," Kim said, looking at the water below.

"Well worth the visit," Katie agreed.

"There are several legends about how this spot got its name," Clint began. "One involves a man named George W. Bonnell, which is most likely the correct one. He was a newspaper editor in New York, and he came to fight in the war against Mexico. He fought the Native Americans, as well He died in 1842, when he was captured and shot by Mexican troops. They named this site in his honor. Another version is a bit more romantic. It involves a couple named Beau and Nell. It says that they were married on this spot just minutes before they were attacked by Indians. After they kissed, they leapt to their deaths before the Indians could capture them. There are other stories involving Native American Princesses and Spanish senoritas, all forced to jump from this spot," Clint said, gesturing with one hand. "Today, it is a popular spot for young lovers to come and see the stars at night."

"Interesting how legends are made," Tom said.

"I think it's quite a romantic spot, don't you?" Amy said, looking sweetly at Tom.

"If you say so," he replied.

Amy's elbow jabbed smartly into his side.

"Ouch," he said, rubbing at the spot.

Just then a loud crash of thunder shook the hill top, quickly followed by a brilliant flash of lightening.

"We'd better head back down the hill before it starts to rain," Clint said, turning around.

They had only made it about a quarter of the way down the steps when the skies opened up and the rain came down in buckets full. Lance grabbed hold of Stormy's arm and guided her down the steps as she pulled her sweater tightly over her body. The rain came down even heavier as they continued, making it harder for them to see the steps. Rivers of muddy water flowed down on both sides of them as they carefully made their way to the bottom of the hill. Near the end, Kim slipped off a muddy step and into the water flowing along one side. She ended up in a muddy pool of water at the bottom of the steps. Kati hurried carefully down the remaining steps and stopped to help her sister up.

"Are you okay, Kim?" Kati asked, worried about the fall.

"I think so, just a little embarrassed and completely covered in mud," she said, her clothes drenched.

"Come on, let's get to the van and back to the hotel," Clint shouted above the next clap of thunder. "We can all change into dry clothes and then see what we might do from there."

Nancy had been waiting at the bottom of the stairs with her umbrella securely over her head in one hand and a crutch tucked firmly under the other arm. When Frank reached the bottom step, she pulled him in underneath the umbrella and hobbled along side him to the waiting

The Austin Fires

van. He started to protest and say he did not need an umbrella, but she would hear nothing of it.

A very interesting woman, Stormy though. *One minute Nancy seems so shy and reserved, and the next, she's a no nonsense woman. I wonder?*

The van arrived back at the Drakeston with a very wet group of passengers, not to mention a very muddy Kim. They went straight to their rooms after being told by Clint that they would gather in about two hours down in the café to decide on their evenings plans.

"It's great to be dry again," Stormy said, drying her hair with a large, soft towel after a nice warm bath.

"Look out the window," Frank told her from across the room. "It has stopped raining and the sun is shining brightly."

"Well, you know what they say about the weather," she said. "You just have to wait five minutes and it'll change. One never knows, and it seems that many weathermen don't either." She laughed and went to put her towel over the rack in the bathroom.

Stormy finished getting dressed for the night's activities and they got ready to leave. Lance had just closed the door behind them after following Stormy out into the hallway, when they heard a loud crash coming from a room down the hall. The two quickly headed in the direction of the noise, arriving in front of a door where they were sure the noise had come from.

"I'm sure this is Amy's room," Stormy whispered.

"Let's have a look and see if she is okay," Lance said, knocking loudly on the door as he called out Amy's name.

"Amy, this is Lance and Stormy. Are you okay?" he called through the door.

There was no answer, and there were no sounds coming from the room. Not hearing a response, Lance tried the doorknob. It was't locked so he turned it and slowly pushed open the door. He and Stormy stepped into the room. As they entered, they were just in time to see a tennis-shoed foot leaving the windowsill and disappearing outside. They dashed over to the far side of the room and looked out the opened window.

"Look," Stormy said, pointing to the fire escape. A man in dark clothing was hurrying down the fire escape ladder. When he reached the end of the ladder, he hung from it momentarily and then jumped the last few feet to the ground below, landing squarely on his feet on the hard pavement. He took off in a full run down the street and around the corner of the building, never once looking back.

"What's going on here?" a stern voice said from behind them.

Lance and Stormy turned around to see Tom standing behind them, his feet planted firmly on the floor, a hard look in his eyes.

"What are you doing in here?" he asked, glaring at the two of them.

"Hi, Tom," Stormy said in what she hoped sounded like a friendly, calm voice. "As we were leaving our room to come downstairs, we heard a crash from this room. We came to investigate the noise and saw that it had come from Amy's room. We were worried about her and wanted to see if she was all right. When we knocked, and she didn't answer, we came in to check on her. Just as

The Austin Fires

we stepped into the room, we caught a glimpse of a foot leaving the window sill."

"We dashed to the window, but were too late to catch the man," Lance continued for her. "He got away down the fire escape and ran around the side of the building."

Tom leaned out the open window. "Well, he's gone now," he said. "I guess there's nothing we can do about it for now. Did you happen to see who it was?"

"No, I'm afraid we didn't," Stormy said.

Just then, Amy entered the room and saw the three of them standing by the window.

"Are we having a party in here and you didn't even invite me?" she asked looking at them, her eyes twinkling.

Stormy quickly related once again what had happened and why they were in Amy's room. Amy eyes clouded over as she looked around the room to see if anything had been taken. Even though she could tell that her things had been gone through, she did not discover anything missing. Stormy suggested that they call the hotel security, but since nothing was missing Amy saw no need for this.

"If they return and try this again, I'll call the hotel security," Amy said. "From now on, I'll secure the windows better when I leave the room. Funny though, I don't remember leaving that window open, but I guess I must have."

Stormy turned back to the window to take a better look at it. There were no marks on the sill or window indicating that it had been forced open.

Maybe Amy did leave it open and just forgot she had, Stormy thought, looking over in Tom's direction, *or maybe someone else opened it to let this guy in.*

After asking Amy if they could do any thing else for her, and the answer being in the negative, Lance and Stormy left the room and took the elevator down to the main floor. On the way down, they discussed what had happened in Amy's room. Stormy took out her pen and small notebook to add it to her growing lists.

"I wonder what that was all about," Lance said. "The guy takes the trouble to break into Amy's room, goes through all of her things, and then doesn't take a thing."

"That does seem odd," she said. "That's, if Amy is telling the truth. Did you notice how nonchalant Tom was acting about someone breaking into his fiancé's room?"

"Yes, now that you mention it," Lance said. "If it had been your room or even mine when I used to go on travel, I would have called for security right away and seen to it that you, or I, were moved to another room."

"I think we need to keep our eyes and ears open a bit wider as to what is going on around here," Stormy said. "I think someone in our party is in danger, and it's getting more serious."

"It sure is beginning to look that way," Lance agreed.

Chapter Twelve

Down stairs, they found Clint in the lobby talking to Frank and Nancy. Kim and Kati were admiring the beautiful paintings and statues along the walls. Lance and Stormy joined Clint and the Thorntons.

"Are you ready to go out to dinner and dancing?" Clint asked them.

"It sounds like fun," Stormy said, "but what about you, Nancy? Surely you could not be out there on the dance floor. Maybe we should consider another activity for tonight where Nancy could enjoy herself too."

"No, it's alright to go dancing," Nancy said. "I will enjoy sitting at one of the tables, listening to the music, and watching the dancers. Let's go tonight."

"Okay, dear," Frank said, "if that's what you want to do."

Okay, folks," Clint said. "We'll keep to the schedule as planned then. Every one to the van please and we'll go on to our reservations at The Oasis. It sits at 450 feet above Lake Travis, and wait until you see the view from there. We should be there before sunset, so you can enjoy how beautiful it looks from up on the hill."

They all climbed into the waiting van and headed out. The traffic was a little heavy on the highways, but it thinned out some as they turned off and made their way up the tree-lined road. They passed several small streams along the side of the roadway. There were horses grazing in green pastures, and large spacious houses were scattered here and there throughout the area.

"This city holds so many surprises around every corner," Stormy said to Lance.

"Yes, it does. I like it here," he replied.

"It's pretty in Los Angeles, but this place has a quaint kind of beauty about it," Amy said.

They arrived at The Oasis to a jam-packed parking lot. The driver had to park the van away from the restaurant on a dirt parking lot. They got out of the van and headed toward the buildings. The entry way was a lovely courtyard filled with statues of animals, people, and a variety of interesting objects. After looking around the courtyard for a while, the group headed through the entry into the restaurant's eating area and heard a band playing lively music from a raised platform.

A young blonde-haired waiter led them to a large table set on one of the restaurants many wooden decks over looking the lake. They were all seated around the table and the waiter took their drink orders. A waitress brought three baskets of chips and several small colorful dishes of salsa to place around their table.

Fans, hung from beams around the decks, cooled off the guests as they enjoyed their dinners. The group

The Austin Fires

noticed though, that if you sat at a table too close to one of these fans, you would have to fight to keep your napkins from blowing away.

"Look at this view," Stormy declared, dipping a chip into a near by salsa bowl.

"What lake is that down below us?" Kim asked Clint, pointing at the large body of water beneath them.

"That's Lake Travis and as I said before, we're sitting 450 feet above its surface," Clint replied. "It's a very popular lake for boating and sailing. This restaurant boasts as many as 40 outdoor decks that look out on the lake, as well as their indoor dining area. I thought we would all like to sit outside on the deck and enjoy the gorgeous sunset The Oasis is famous for."

The group enjoyed the lively music played by the country band as the waiter delivered their drinks and took their food orders. The sun was just setting as their orders arrived. The sky was filled with a bright array of colors. Red, orange, yellow, green, blue, and purple blended across the horizon to delight the most avid artistic soul.

"What a wonderful setting this is," Stormy said, looking around the place, "and live music, too."

"The food's good, too," Lance said, taking another bite.

"Yeah, isn't it great," Amy said, tapping her foot to the beat of the music. "Let's go out there and dance to this song, Tom."

"I'm still eating, Amy," Tom said. "Maybe ... What?"

Amy grabbed Tom's arm before he could finish his sentence and wouldn't take no for an answer. She dragged him out on the dance floor. Tom scowled for a few minutes, but then a big smile broke out across his face. He seemed to be having a good time out there after all. They both could dance quite well and made a good pair together, Stormy noticed.

After Lance had finished his meal, he stood up, and bowed to Stormy.

"May I have this dance, my dear?" he asked, his eyes twinkling.

"Why surely, my good man," she returned, her own blue eyes lighting up. They danced off into the crowd.

Back at the table, Nancy encouraged Frank to dance with the sisters, taking them out onto the dance floor. He finally agreed to the idea and the sisters eagerly took him up on his offer. Clint jumped up and went out to the floor with them as well.

Stormy and Lance returned to the table after a few dances, sitting down beside Nancy.

"It's been a while since we've been dancing," Stormy said, a little short of breath. "It sure was a lot of fun out there though."

"Yes," Lance said, taking a drink of his soda. "We'll have to go out for more dancing when we get back home to Phoenix."

"Do you like living in Phoenix?" Nancy asked them.

"Yes, we do" Stormy replied, "but the hot summers are getting a little hard to take as I get older."

"I like the heat," Lance said. "The roses do quite well there."

The Austin Fires

"It's a little hard on my vegetable garden though especially in the hottest part of the summer," Stormy said. "How is it where you live in Atlanta, Nancy?"

"We love it," Nancy said. "Though as you've probably heard, it gets very humid in the summer time there, but you get used to it. We take lots of showers, too," she laughed.

"What does Frank like to do now that he's retired from the railroad?" Lance asked Nancy.

"More trains, of course," Nancy said. "He's building a large miniature village in our spare room with lots of different kinds of trains. He has little trees, buildings, and lots of people all doing various things about the town. He even has some little dogs and cats running throughout the neighborhoods. It takes up a lot of his time, so we don't get to go out too many places together any more. He's always running off here and there buying new stuff for his village. That is why I finally gave in to my friends' suggestion that I open a craft shop together with her. Frank thought it was a good idea. I was surprised when out of the blue Frank suggested we come on this tour. It's so unlike him."

"Well maybe he thought it was a good way to make up for spending so much time on his trains," Stormy said, as the waiter refilled her water glass and added fresh lemon slices to it.

"Maybe," Nancy said, seeming lost in thought.

"Wow, these girls are wearing me out," Frank shouted, sitting down heavily in the chair next to Nancy. "I can hardly keep up with them."

"Oh, he did just fine," Kati said. "He was dancing rings around me."

"Yes," Kim said. "He's quite a good dancer. Much better than Clint, but don't mention I said that."

"No, we won't," Stormy said, feigning seriousness.

Frank beamed at the sister's compliments, taking a big gulp from his glass of lemonade. Stormy saw a disturbing look momentarily flash across Nancy's face and then disappear. She wondered what that meant.

Tom and Amy returned to the table, with Clint not far behind them. They all ordered dessert, chatting about various things while they ate it. Stormy thought her pie alamode was very good. She was really enjoying the evening.

After dessert, they piled back into the van and returned to the hotel. Tom and Amy opted to go to a dance club down the street, and Kim and Katie, accompanied by Clint, enthusiastically went along.

"How about going on an evening carriage ride, Storm?" Lance asked.

"Oh, Lance, that would be wonderful!" Stormy said, her blue eyes filled with excitement. "I've seen them in the streets here, and you know how much I've always wanted to go on one."

"I know. We'll ask the hotels' concierge where we can catch the carriages," he said. "Wait here and I'll go see."

He dashed inside the hotel, leaving Stormy standing on the side walk with Frank and Nancy.

"Frank, why don't we go for a ride in a carriage, too," Nancy asked her husband. "It sounds like a lot of fun."

"Well, I don't know with your leg and all," he said, uncertainly.

"I'll be sitting in the carriage, not pulling it," Nancy said, rolling her eyes at her husband.

Lance returned, saying that the carriage stop was just around the corner from the hotel. The hotel's front desk had called the carriage service and a rig would be arriving at the stop in approximately fifteen minutes.

"Good, that will give me a few minutes to run upstairs to our room and grab a coat," Stormy said. "It's a little chilly out."

"Hurry back," Lance said. "We don't want to miss the carriage in case it arrives early."

"I promise I'll hurry," she said as she dashed through the hotel's front door.

"Okay, Nancy, I'll see," Frank said, turning around to face Lance.

"Do you think we might hitch a ride with you in the carriage that's coming?" Frank asked.

"Well," Lance hesitated, trying to think of an excuse to say no. "I'll have to check with Stormy when she comes back."

"I'll pay for half the cost and throw in the tip as well," Frank bellowed out.

Upstairs, Stormy stepped off the elevator and out into the hallway. Heading in the direction of her room, she spotted a figure in dark clothes wearing a black baseball cap pulled down low over its face emerge from a doorway from down at the end of the hall. The figure turned in Stormy's direction and spotted her in the hallway. It stood still for a moment, then turned and hurried toward the stairs at the other end of the hall, disappearing through the stairwell door.

"That's weird," Stormy said aloud to herself. "What strange behavior. It's almost as if the person didn't want me to see who they are."

She hurried to the end of the hall and slowly opened the stairwell door. Stepping onto the landing, she looked over the stair rail and down below. She spotted the figure stepping quickly through the doorway leading to the floor beneath her, the door shutting with a bang behind it.

Stormy went back through the door and into the hallway. She went to look at the room number of the door where she had seen the figure emerge. She was surprised to see that the room was Tom's.

"I wonder who that was and what they were doing in Tom's room?" she said. "And, if Tom knows that they were in there?"

Stormy hurried to her room, used the bathroom, and grabbed a light coat from the closet. She stepped into the hallway and shut the door securely behind her. Looking around the hall once more, and finding it empty, she rushed to the elevator and down to the main floor.

Chapter Thirteen

"Just in time, Stormy," Lance said, taking her by the arm and hurrying her along. "I can hear the clip-clop of the horse coming down the street. The Thorntons are waiting at the carriage stop for us. I hope you don't mind if they come with along."

"Oh, I thought we were going alone," Stormy said, surprised and a little disappointed.

"Yes, we were," Lance said, lowering his voice as they turned the corner of the building, "but Nancy wanted to go, also, and this was the only carriage they had available for over an hour. Frank was very insistent and I felt sorry for Nancy."

"That's nice of you, Lance," Stormy said, patting his arm. "It would have been more romantic with out them, but it's okay if they come."

They joined Frank and Nancy as a beautiful shiny white carriage, with deep-blue velvet seats and matching interior side panels, pulled by an equally striking black draft horse came to a stop in front of them. The driver atop the carriage seat looked stunning in his old fashion livery outfit, including tails and a black top hat.

"Good evening, madams and sirs," the driver addressed them with a slight bow. "Are you the party that called for my carriage?"

"Yes, we are," Lance said. "I hope it will be okay for our friends here to join us for the ride?"

"Of course, Sir, I am driving the larger carriage this evening, and there is plenty of room for all of you," he said, climbing down from his seat. He opened the carriages' side door, lowered a few metal steps, and bowed to the ladies.

"Thank you," Lance replied.

"Watch your step as you climb in, please. Let me help you, madam," the driver said, taking hold of Nancy's arm and helping her up into the coach.

Frank handed up the crutch he had been holding for his wife. Next, the driver helped Stormy into the carriage. Frank and Lance climbed up and took their places beside the women.

After all were seated comfortably on the soft blue velvet seats, each couple on a side facing the other, the driver leapt to the coaches' top seat and settled in. He took the horse's reins in hand, and with a click of his tongue said, "Off we go now, Nickers. Let's give these nice folks a good ride around the town."

The four-some enjoyed themselves as the carriage slowly made its way along the streets of down town Austin at a rate of not more than five miles an hour, Lance estimated when Nancy asked how fast they were traveling. The slow pace gave them plenty of time to look over the sights and discuss what they saw. A few people walking down the sidewalks waved and smiled to the group as the horse and carriage passed them by. They waved and smiled back in return.

"Oh, this is so much fun," Stormy said to Lance. "I feel like a princess waving to the commoners along the streets of London."

"No, not a princess," Lance said, taking her hand and kissing it, "but a queen, my dear."

"Oh, Lance," Stormy said, smiling, "you are so sweet."

They continued through the streets, one after another, enjoying each new one even more than the one before it. Frank seemed to be whispering things into Nancy's ear now and then producing a smile upon her face.

I didn't think he knew how to speak in any thing other than a loud voice, Stormy mused, looking over at the two sitting close together.

She looked at Lance next to her and found that he, too, was looking in the direction of Frank and Nancy. Lance turned and looked at Stormy, shrugging his shoulders. He was obviously thinking the same thoughts as she was. They shared a quiet laugh together.

Stormy pulled back the cuff of her blouse and looked at her wristwatch. They still had fifteen minutes of their hours' ride to go. She wished this could last forever. She was greatly enjoying the evening when she noticed a large group of people up ahead of them exiting a theater and crowding onto the sidewalk as they chatted excitedly with one another. As the carriage drew closer, she was about to point this group out to Lance and ask him if he had heard of the production that was listed on the marquee above the theater doors, when suddenly a darkly dressed figure stepped from the crowd and threw a lit fire cracker behind their horse's back hooves. Just as quickly as the figure had appeared, it disappeared back into the crowd and was gone. The startled horse reared back and struck its hooves into the air. It reared again and bolted at a dead run down the black pavement, pulling the carriage behind it at neck breaking speed.

"Whoa… Nickers… whoa," the driver yelled to the wide-eyed horse. "It's okay, fella, whoa."

The driver held onto the reins with all his might, trying to control the horse as it dashed in and out of the cars around it in the street. Frightened pedestrians dove out of the way as the horse and carriage flew on toward them.

"Hold on to the rails tightly," Lance yelled, grabbing onto Stormy's arm to keep her from being flung from the carriage. They all took his advice and hung on as tightly as they could. Frank held onto Nancy as they slid this way and that across the carriage seat.

"Nickers stop, whoa, whoa, boy" the driver continued to shout at the run away horse as he pulled back on the reins. He did his best to keep the carriage from over turning.

The group continued to hang onto what ever they could as the wild ride continued to take them further and further down the streets, narrowly missing colliding with one car after another.

Nancy's crutch suddenly flew from the carriage out into the middle of the street, but no one dared to try and stop it for fear of falling out with it. Stormy prayed that the horse would soon tire out and stop, or some kind of

The Austin Fires

help would arrive soon. She doubted that she could hang on much longer. Most likely, none of them could.

As if in answer to her prayer, a police car came up beside the run away horse, and passed it by. The car carefully turned in front of the horse, slowing the horse's pace down a little. A second police car came up beside the carriage on their left, and a third car closed in on their right side. In a well-orchestrated movement, they boxed the horse and carriage in between them and slowed it down, finally causing the horse to come to a complete stop.

"Thank goodness," Stormy said relieved, relaxing her grip on the carriages sidebars.

The tired out horse stood still, trying to catch its breath, its sides heaving in an out. The driver, after checking to make sure his passengers were alright, jumped to the ground and went to the horse's side, in an attempt to further calm the horse and assess the damage.

"Wow, what a ride," Frank shouted, pale as a ghost.

"I'm surprised we're still in one piece," his wife said, still holding onto the sides of the carriage with whitened knuckles.

"Me, too," Stormy said, a bit shaken.

"Yes, that was more than we signed up for," Lance put in.

"It's a good thing the driver is so skilled with his horse," Frank said, shaking his head. "I don't know what that person was thinking to run out in front of the horse and scare him like they did."

"That was just plain mean," Stormy said. "Why would they do such a thing?"

"Who knows," Lance replied, helping Stormy down from the carriage, "but I'm glad the cavalry showed up when it did. Even if they came in cars."

The police questioned them all and took down their statements, including where they were staying for further possible questioning. It was getting late when they were finished, and the driver told them the company would send out another horse and carriage to take them back to their hotel.

"Nickers is through for the night," the driver said, patting the damp side of the black horse affectionately.

The group thanked the driver, but opted to take a taxi instead.

Back at the hotel, they headed straight for their rooms. All were exhausted after their ordeal.

Once in their own room, Stormy and Lance discussed the wild ride as they got ready for bed.

"Wow, that's a ride I'll never forget," Stormy said. "I don't understand why that person did such a horrible thing by spooking the horse the way they did."

"Yes, that was a terrible thing to do for sure," Lance said, hanging up Stormy's coat for her in the closet. "With only the vague description we could give the police there is not much chance of them ever finding out who he or she was."

"You know, the shape of that figure looked similar to the man I saw in the hallway today, come to think of it" she said, brushing her blonde hair in even strokes.

"What man?" Lance asked, unbuttoning the last button on his shirt and slipping it off.

"When I came up to get my coat before we went on the carriage ride, I saw a man coming out of Tom's room.

The Austin Fires

He turned to head my way at first, but when he saw me, he stopped, turned the other way, and quickly headed for the stairs," Stormy said. "I'm sure he saw me quite clearly, but he wore a dark long sleeved shirt and long pants with a cap pulled down low over his head. I didn't get much of a look at him, I'm sorry to say."

"If he was up to no good here maybe he followed us and tried to throw you off his path, so to speak," Lance said. "No pun intended," he added when she sighed at him.

Stormy took out her little note book and a pen from her purse and added this latest incident to her growing lists. She read back through her notes and then sat there for a few minutes, thinking things through.

"You know, Lance," she said, flipping through the pages of her notebook, "I think things are starting to form a pattern. Some of them are connecting together and they are beginning to point to a few people on my lists more than any of the others. I wonder… hmmm."

"Who do you think it points to and why?" he asked her, now very curious.

"Let me think about it a little longer before I say it out loud," she replied. "I want to check over a few things to be sure. I think we should stay very alert though."

"Okay, well let's go to bed. We can add tonight's incident to the computer list tomorrow. We'll keep our eyes open tomorrow and see what we can find," Lance suggested. "What's on the agenda for tomorrow?"

"Let me look at the list," Stormy replied. Picking up the packet of papers off the nearby chair, which the tour guide had given them, she folded over the schedule to the following page and checked the next day's activities.

"It says TBD on the list for tomorrow," she read, "so I guess we'll have to wait until the morning to find out."

"Okay, let's turn out the lights and get to bed," he mumbled, half asleep already.

"All right, in just a moment. I want to read a few paragraphs first," Stormy said. "I'm still a little keyed up, and it will help me to calm down."

When there was no response from Lance, she looked over in the direction of the bed. Lance lay under the covers softly snoring, fast asleep. She doubted he had even heard any of her last few remarks.

Well, let him sleep, she thought. *It's been quite a day. I'll just read for a couple of minutes and then join him for a good nights sleep.*

Stormy finished brushing her hair and put the brush away on the bathroom counter. She retrieved her book from the nightstand next to the bed and went to sit in the same cozy chair she had sat in a few nights before. The light from the gooseneck lamp next to the chair was perfect for reading and in turn would not disturb Lance's sleep. Soon she was completely absorbed in her mystery book.

Chapter Fourteen

Some time later, she was aware of a noise out in the hall. She put her book down, crept to the door, and listened closely. She definitely heard voices and they were getting closer. As she continued to listen, she was sure she heard Tom's voice and that of Amy's'. Added to theirs were the voices of Kim and Kati.

I guess they finally made it back from the dance club, thought Stormy.

She returned to her chair, picked up her book, and was soon engrossed in it once again.

After what seemed like only a short time had passed, she again heard noises from out in the hallway. She put her book down once more, rose from her chair, and quietly crept to the door. She placed her ear to the door's smooth surface and listened intently. The noises from the hall were very soft and subtle, not like someone just going to their room for the night, as the others had done. The more Stormy listened, the more curious she became.

Suddenly there was a loud grinding noise from further down the hall. Next, she heard footsteps slowly going back down the hall. She waited for a few minutes to make sure that all was quiet and that there was less chance of someone still being out in the hall way.

Stormy quietly unlocked the door and slowly pulled it open a small crack from which she peered out. Seeing no one nearby, she opened it wider and carefully looked both ways down the hall. She thought she saw a shadow near the elevator doors as they closed. The elevator chimed and was on its way down by the time she reached it. Stormy patiently stood still and watched the numbers change on the indicator above its doors until it showed that the elevator had come to a stop.

"It stopped in the basement?" she questioned. "Who would be going down there at this time of night? Further more, why would they be going there at all? I'm sure there aren't any rooms down there."

Stormy ran back to her room and quietly walked over to the night stand on the side of the bed. Lance continued to snore, deep in a peaceful sleep. She knew he would not like her going out without him this time of night, but since he was sleeping ever so nicely she decided not to wake him up.

She hurriedly wrote him a quick note telling him she would be right back. At the top of the note she wrote down the time she had left the room. This was something they had always done to keep each other informed, and it was old habit by now.

Grabbing the small flashlight from out of her purse, which she always carried with her, and throwing on her heavier bathrobe and shoes, Stormy went to the door. Here

The Austin Fires

she hesitated, turned around, and crossed the room to the wall by the balcony doors. She grabbed the walking stick leaning up against it, just in case, and quietly returned to the door and stepped from the room. Closing the door behind her, she headed for the elevators. Upon reaching it, she stopped before pushing the call button.

"I think it would be a better idea to use the stairs in this case," Stormy whispered to herself. "That way, if someone is still down in the basement, and any where near the elevator, they'll not know I'm coming or hear the noise of the elevator at all."

She headed back for the stairs and slowly opened the door to the stairwell. The stairs were well lit so there was no need for her to use the flashlight she had brought with her. Carefully holding her stick in front of her, she went through the door and down the stairs as quietly, but as quickly as she could, not wishing to alert anyone that might possibly be on the stairs below her. Especially if that shadowy figure she saw by the elevator had decided to use the stairs to come back up from the basement instead of riding the elevator again.

After passing through a few stair landings and stepping down too many stairs to count, she reached the door that led into the basement. Ever so carefully, Stormy pulled open the door. It made a small creaking noise, but hopefully not loud enough to alert anyone of her presence. She stepped out into the basement's hallway. At first, she could barely see down the hallway in either direction as it was poorly lit, but after a few minutes her eyes began to adjust.

There were several doors along each side of the hallway to the left of her and again to the right. All of them appeared to be closed with no light of any kind coming from beneath a single one.

Well, who ever rode the elevator down here must be gone by now, she thought, *but I think I should have a quick look around anyway.*

Stormy decided to start down the hallway to the right of the stairs. As she reached each door, she quickly examined and tried its door knob to see if any of them were unlocked. After reaching the far end of the hall, she turned around and headed back toward the stairs, checking each of the doors she came to in case one of them might be unlocked. Finding not one of the doors accessible on either side of the hallway, she started down the hall on the left side. Using the same method of checking as she had done on the right side, she made her way down the hall, stopping at each door and checking each knob. Not one of them budged.

Even though she was getting discouraged, Stormy pressed on. Arriving at the end of this hallway she tried the last door before starting back again on the other side of the hall. She was surprised to find that this doors' knob turned easily in her hand. She stopped and looked back down the hall. Not seeing anyone in sight, Stormy turned back again to the unlocked door. Slowly she turned the knob and opened the door.

Stormy was surprised to find that a light was on in the room. It was filled with many boxes piled high on top of each other in several rows. To the left side of the room she saw what appeared to be a long workbench running along much of the wall. Over to the right of the door were a mop and two brooms leaning in the corner of the wall.

The Austin Fires

She could not tell how far back the room went with all those boxes in the way.

She carefully stepped through the door as quietly as she could. Softly closing the door behind her and leaning on her stick, she stood there and listened some more.

It won't hurt to take just a quick look around before I head back to my room, Stormy thought.

She decided she would check out the worktable first to see just what kind of work was done in this room.

Maybe this is the janitors' closet or his workroom, Stormy wondered.

Heading toward the table, she came to a sudden stop. A small noise was coming from behind the boxes. She was sure something or someone had moved behind them.

Curiosity getting the better of her, Stormy turned and headed for the other end of the room to take a peak and see what she could find. Hoping there would be a janitor who was taking inventory of the supplies or had laid down for a quick nap before returning back to work and not some maniac, she continued. If he saw her, he would probably be angry and wonder why she was here where she did not belong.

Maybe I'd had better leave now and go back to my room, she thought. *No, I have to at least take a quick look first.*

She decided to proceed quietly and then creep out the door before she was spotted.

Slowly she crept around the boxes only to discover even more boxes. They were piled just as high as the front row had been. Continuing beyond these, she finally came to the back wall of the room. Here a narrow aisle formed between the boxes and the wall. Stormy carefully made her way down the aisle stepping as softly as she could and listening for anyone else who might be in the room with her.

She had made her way to about half way down the narrow aisle when suddenly a noise came from the other side of the boxes she was passing. Her attention was drawn toward the top of the stack just in time to see them falling down toward where she was standing. There was no time for her to get out of the way, so Stormy squatted down against the wall and holding her stick in both hands, held it tightly over her head.

Down came the boxes upon her like a ton of bricks. From across the room a door opened and slammed quickly shut again. The sound of a key being put into a lock and being turned, told her this wasn't just an accident.

Someone had been in the room with me, Stormy thought, trying to get her breath back into her empty lungs. *How am I going to get out from under all of these boxes?*

Pushing at the boxes that lay piled on top of her with the aid of her walking stick, she was surprised to find that most of them were light in weight, some even appearing to be empty. As she continued moving the boxes to one side of her, she was finally able to see the ceiling above.

Stormy sat up and eventually made her way onto her feet. Feeling a little dizzy at first, she decided to take it slowly. Steadying herself against the wall with one hand and her stick in the other, she stood there for a few minutes, regaining both her breath and her strength.

"Well, there goes another lost B vitamin," she laughed to herself.

After a few moments she felt much better. With the dizziness gone and her strength returning, she began wading through the sea of boxes in front of her. She

The Austin Fires

picked up each box in front of her and carefully tossed it over her head on the stack behind. As she made her way Stormy stopped and examined a box or two, curious as to what was in them. Some of the labels read "Toilet Tissue" while others said "Paper Towels".

"No wonder they are so light weight. Good thing these boxes didn't have cleaning supplies or books in them," Stormy said, rubbing the top of her head. "My head would have hurt a lot more than it does right now. And I could imagine what my children would say if I got knocked out by a few rolls of toilet paper."

Chapter Fifteen

Finally, after much struggling and shifting around of the boxes, she came around the first row which was still standing in tall, neat piles. Beyond that she saw the work bench area of the room. Everything looked okay in this area, with no fallen boxes. She turned and headed for the door, hoping she was wrong in what she had heard earlier.

"Darn, I guess I was right. Locked in," she said, turning the doorknob back and forth with her hand to no avail. "Someone wanted to make sure I couldn't, or wouldn't, follow them. Now what should I do?"

She examined the door and noticed that the door's hinges were on the inside of the room.

"Great, there's a chance," Stormy said, relieved.

She looked around the room until her gaze come to rest upon the workbench.

"Surely they would keep some tools on a workbench," Stormy said aloud as she headed in the direction of the bench. Upon reaching it, she saw that it was covered with several jars holding an assortment of nails, screws, and nuts. Next to them on the table, she noticed a large circular saw accompanied by plenty of sawdust. Over to one side of the bench she saw several wooden drawers. She opened each of the drawers in turn and rummaged through them. Not a screwdriver in sight.

"What kind of a workbench is this without any tools to be had?" Stormy said, exasperated.

She turned around and looked at the wall on the other side of the room. Once again, her eye caught the mops and brooms leaning up against the wall and she crossed the room to where they stood.

"Ah, what's behind here?" Stormy said, pushing aside a mop.

A small alcove had been placed in the wall above them and was filled with various cleaning fluids.

"Well, these are of no use unless I want to clean up in here while I wait to be rescued," she quipped, replacing the mop she had moved. "Wait, what's this?"

Stormy spied a small shelf over to one side and slightly above the alcove, fastened tightly against the wall. It was partially hidden behind the remaining mops, brooms, and other assorted cleaning devices. Pushing them aside, she found what looked to be an old hammer lying in the dust upon the shelf. It looked as if it had been there for some time. Picking it up, she found that the hammer's head was a little rusty and the wood of its handle had been shattered part way down. As she examined it further, a sliver of wood jabbed into her index finger.

"Ouch! This must be quite old," Stormy said, pulling the splinter from the throbbing finger, "but it might just

The Austin Fires

do the trick. But it will need a few repairs before it can be used."

Stormy took the hammer with her back to the workbench and set it down. She turned toward the drawers and opened the top one. Reaching inside, she pulled out the roll of gray duct tape that she had spotted earlier. Unrolling the tape, she proceeded to wrap the handle of the old hammer tightly with tape along the entire length of the wood. She wrapped it twice in hopes of making it stronger and more secure.

"There," she said, smoothing out the tape along the handle with her hand. "It should be much easier to use now."

Knowing that the hammer alone would not get her out of the room, Stormy continued to search the room for more usable items. She was starting to give up hope of finding what she wanted, when she spied a shiny object under the far end of the bench. Bending down to the floor, she reached back as far as she could in an attempt to retrieve it.

"I'm glad I remembered my walking stick," Stormy said. "It comes in handy for many otherwise unreachable things in life."

She retrieved her stick from where she had left it leaning against the wall and tried again to reach the object on the floor. This time she was successful in her attempt and dragged it out from under the bench, picking up the object with her other hand. On examining it closer, she found it was just what she needed for her escape from this basement tomb. A long, heavy metal nail.

"Perfect!" she cried.

Taking the nail and the hammer to the door, Stormy studied the doors' hinges up close.

"Okay, it might just work," she said.

Remembering what Lance had taught her about hanging doors when they had screened in their back porch last summer, she placed the long nail on the under side of the door's bottom hinge pin first and positioned the hammer beneath the nail. She proceeded to pound the nail carefully upward against the pin, taking care not to smash her knuckles on the floor below.

It took a bit of hammering, but Stormy finally managed to knock the pin loose from its hinge. Setting the pin on the floor beside her, she proceeded to the door's middle hinge pin and set to work hammering it out, once again with the long nail she had found. She was able to hammer this pin about half way out when it would move no further.

"Now what's wrong with this one," she said, as she tried to dislodge it.

No matter how hard she struck the nail, it would not budge. It was stuck fast in the hinge. On examining it closer, she could not see anything that might be holding it from moving further.

"I know, I need some sort of lubricant to get this thing moving. What is there around here that would do the trick?"

Looking around the room once again and spotting the shelf full of cleaners, she walked over to it. She searched the shelf, examining each of the containers. She could see nothing on the shelf that would help to lubricate the pin. The hinge and pin would be very shiny if she used some of the container's contents, but she did not think it would not enable her to get the pin out of its hinge.

Walking back toward the rows of boxes that were still stacked upright, she examined the ones in front of her.

"What's in this one?" she wondered, spotting a label on one of the boxes near her part way up in the stack. Moving closer to the box, she read its label. The word 'Olive Oil' was clearly printed on its side.

"Great! This will do just fine," Stormy said, carefully removing the box from the stack and setting it on the floor beneath. Ripping open the box and reaching inside, she pulled forth a large bottle of Italy's finest and headed back to the door.

She removed the bottle's cover and slowly poured the olive oil down in the top of the hinge where the pin was stuck tight. The oil flowed down the entire length of the hinge and dripped out from the bottom. Once again she placed the large nail against the pin and whacked it with the old hammer. This time it moved a small amount. Overjoyed, she continued to hit the nail with the hammer until the pin came loose from the hinge and she could pull it easily out from the top. Tossing it aside with the first pin, she applied the olive oil to the doors' last hinge at the top of the door before she tried hammering it at all. After several good whacks with the hammer, the pin came out and she removed it as well.

"Okay, now let's see if I can knock this door loose from these hinges with out the whole thing falling in on me," Stormy said.

She began pounding on the hinges and eventually they came loose. Using the broken claw of the old hammer, she separated the hinges and the door came off.

It was none too soon for as she loosened the last hinge the hammerhead broke off from the handle and fell to the floor beneath her feet. It felt to Stormy as if the hammer had given its life, its last breath, to save her from rotting away in this basement storeroom.

Setting the remains of the hammer onto the floor next to the discarded pins and getting a better grip on the door, she slowly dragged it over to the wall beside her. Leaning it against the wall, she returned to the now open doorway and carefully looked out of the room. Spotting no one lurking in the hallway, she grabbed her stick and stepped from the room carefully making her way to the elevator. This time she would not creep around the stairs. She would take the elevator up to her floor and go straight to her room and a sleeping Lance.

It had been a couple of hours since she'd left her room to follow the mysterious shadow of a person down to the basement. She hoped to sneak back into her hotel room and climb into bed with out waking Lance.

When the elevator doors opened at her floor, all her hopes were dashed. There, standing outside of the elevator staring back at her, was Lance with a worried look across his face. Next to him stood Amy and Tom, looking more annoyed than worried.

"Where have you been?" yelled Lance as Stormy stepped out of the elevator, "and at this time of night? I've been worried sick about you."

"Um, I couldn't sleep so I walked around the hotel for a while," she replied, looking over at Tom. He was scowling once again. "Sorry to have worried you," she said, looking back at Lance.

The Austin Fires

"Well come on. Let's get you back to the room," Lance said. Turning toward Tom and Amy, he added, "Thanks for your help. Sorry to have disturbed you so late."

"No problem at all," Amy said, a smile playing about her face.

Tom and Amy turned away and walked down the hall way as Lance escorted Stormy back to their own room.

Once inside after shutting and relocking the door it was time for twenty questions. Stormy sat down heavily upon the edge of the bed. Removing her slippers, she rubbed her tired feet.

"What on earth is going on, Storm," Lance said, sitting next to her on the bed. "I woke up to find that you were not any where in the room or even in the bathroom. I finally spotted your note. I saw that you had put the time you left at its top, as you usually do, but that was hours ago. Where were you for so long? And what are all these black marks on the palms of your hands?" he added, taking her left hand in his to examine it more closely.

"Well, after you'd fallen asleep and I was reading for a while in that chair, I heard a strange noise outside in the hallway. It was similar to the sounds I heard the other night that I told you about. I carefully opened the door and…." Stormy went on to relate all that she had done and heard, ending with how she had escaped from the basement room.

"What did you think you were doing going after someone this late at night, and alone for that matter?" Lance said, sternly. "You could have been badly injured, or worse, killed by a mad man. Next time, if there is one, and you want to go sleuthing, I want you to wake me up no matter what time it is. Understand?"

"Yes, Lance, I'll wake you up," she replied, "but with so many strange things going on, I wanted to see if I could get a good look at who ever it was that's been sneaking around the hall ways. I hoped it would shed some light on what has been going on around here."

"Maybe it would have, but it was not a very smart way of going about it, Storm," Lance said, looking much calmer now.

"I'm very tired, so how about a few hours of sleep before the sun comes up and we start another day of touring," Stormy said, yawning as she lay back on the bed with a contented sigh.

"You do look like you need a good rest after your ordeal," Lance said, tucking her in under the sheet and blanket, "but please be more careful from now on. I would hate to lose you."

"Okay, dear. I'll try to," Stormy said, drifting off to sleep.

Chapter Sixteen

Later that morning when Stormy awoke, she felt the aches and pains of the previous night's adventure throughout her body. She would have to be more careful from now on. She wasn't as young as she used to be.

There was a knock on the door and Lance came out of the bathroom in time to answer it. Stormy could hear a man's voice speaking with Lance and then the clatter of wheels as Lance rolled a cloth-covered cart into the room, shutting the room's door behind him. He proceeded to roll the cart to a nearby table. Removing the cloth covering with a flourish, he revealed two trays packed full of dishes, each with a beautiful cover on top of it. Stormy's mouth watered and her stomach grumbled at the smells that floated across the room.

"Hope you're hungry, my dear," Lance said, removing the covers and picking up a tray from off the cart. He carried it to where Stormy now sat up in bed, upright against several pillows, and placed it on her lap.

"Oh, Lance, how thoughtful of you to do such a thing," Stormy said, looking over the tray filled with pancakes topped with luscious strawberries and whipped cream, browned sausages and bacon, fluffy scrambled eggs, and a tall glass of cool orange juice. "I've not had breakfast in bed for such a long time."

Lance retrieved a similar tray from the cart and sat in a chair close by Stormy near the bed. His tray was piled with the same delicious items as hers, except he had opted for the French toast and blueberries with cream. They ate in silence for a while, enjoying the wonderful foods as the beautiful music of the song birds out on the balcony filtered in through the open glass doors.

"Thank you, Lance," Stormy said, placing her empty tray along side of her on the bed. "That was a wonderful breakfast and a great treat to have it served to me in bed."

"You are quite welcome, my dear," Lance replied, getting to his feet. "May I take your tray for you?"

"Yes, thank you," she said, handing him the tray. "It sounds like it will be a beautiful day judging from the sound of the birds singing outside."

"It sure is. There's not a cloud in the sky in sight today," Lance said. "Just warm sunshine and plenty of birds, besides the people out and about."

"Have you heard what the tour group is planning for today?" she asked, throwing back the covers and climbing out of bed.

"They were still discussing it when I went down to order breakfast to be sent up to our room," Lance said, throwing his arms around her waist. "Yes, I know, I could've ordered it over the phone, but I wanted to go and

The Austin Fires

see what the plans were for today," he hurried on before she could ask the question 'why'. "There was some talk of a door being removed from off its' hinges somewhere down in the hotel's basement." He grinned at Stormy as a look of chagrin passed over her face.

"I guess I had better go and explain that to the hotel's management this morning," Stormy said. "They'll probably find plenty of my fingerprints around the room and on that door any way. Let me just take a quick shower and change first. I'd also like to add a few quick notes on your lap top to my list, if I may."

"Of course, go ahead," Lance replied, wheeling the breakfast cart over by the door.

When Stormy had showered and changed, she grabbed her walking stick and she and Lance headed down in the elevator to find the hotel managers' office. They enquired at the hotels' front desk if they might see the manager, and were led down a short hallway to a large intricately carved wooden door. After knocking and receiving the okay to enter, the desk clerk let them into the room, then softly closed the door behind and left.

Stormy took note of how large the office was and how beautifully it had been furnished. She felt as if she had stepped back into time. All of the pieces of furniture around the room must have been originals from back in the early days of the hotel, from the 1800's. Even the massive desk across the room looked to be as old as the rest of the pieces. She noticed that they were all in remarkably good repair.

Behind the desk, sat a nice looking man of about 45 or so. He wore his light brown hair in a neat short cut and a nicely trimmed mustache framed his upper lip. His tan shirt had a western cut to it and was nicely complimented by the bolo tie, made of silver and turquoise, hanging around his neck.

"What can I do for you folks?" he said, getting to his feet and offering his hand to them. "I am Jeff Sams, the Drakeston's manager."

"Hello, Mr. Sams, I'm Lance Winters," Lance said, shaking the manager's hand, "and this is my wife, Stormy. We thought you would like to hear what we know about the incident last night with that door down in your basement."

"Yes, I would at that, Mr. Winters," Mr. Sams said. "Will you both please sit down," he said, offering them the two cocoa–colored leather chairs sitting in front of his desk.

"Late last night, my wife heard noises out in the hallway not far from our door," Lance began, looking over at Stormy. "She had heard them before, so she decided to investigate.

"What kind of noises?" Mr. Sams said, leaning forward in his chair and placing his arms on the massive desk. "Go on."

Stormy related to the manager what the noises she heard had sounded like and how often she had heard them. She told him of how she had seen a darkly dressed figure getting into the elevator so late last night and of that person going down to the basement level.

"I was very curious as to why someone would be down there so late," Stormy said, "and since I have been hearing these strange noises, I decided to follow them and find out who it was and why they were there."

The Austin Fires

"We have people on our staff that work all hours of the day and the night, Mrs. Winters," Mr. Sams told her. "If you were concerned, why didn't you call the front desk and report your concerns to them?"

"My wife reads mystery books and likes to try and solve things herself," Lance said, smiling over at Stormy. "I guess she just got carried away."

"I guess so," Stormy said, throwing a questioning look Lance's way. "I'll call the front desk the next time I hear any strange noises." She then proceeded to tell the hotel's manager what had happened down in the basement and why the door ended up off its hinges.

"I'm very sorry that you were locked in that way, Mrs. Winters," Mr. Sams apologized. "It was an unfortunate accident and I'll look into who was on duty last night and recommend that they pay more attention to what they are doing from now on." Opening a top drawer in his desk, he pulled forth two slips of paper which he handed over to Stormy. "Please accept these dinner vouchers for the hotel's dining room as an apology for any inconvenience last night's episode may have caused you." Standing up, he ushered them to the door. "Thank you for letting me know what happened to the door in the basement and I hope you'll enjoy the rest of your stay with us here at the Drakeston." He closed the door behind them, leaving them alone in the hall.

"Well, that was very weird," Stormy said, as she turned and walked down the hall, walking stick in hand, toward the hotel's lobby. "You would think that he would be a little more concerned about people having boxes dumped on their heads and guests being locked in basement rooms.

And what was that you said to him about me getting carried away because I read mystery books all about?"

"Now calm down, Storm," Lance said, as they headed toward two comfortable chairs in the lobby. "Let's sit down here for a few minutes before we look for the others."

Stormy sat down in one of the soft red chairs while Lance took the other one as he explained his comment to the manager.

"I said that about you and the mystery books because I thought it would be better if he just thought of you as a nosy guest looking for a mystery to solve. I didn't think it was a good idea to tell him about all of the other strange things that have been going on, and I'm not sure he would want to know any way. He was trying to make light of the whole thing and this seemed to smooth it over for him," Lance said. "Who knows, he may have even charged us for the door other wise," he said, a smile on his lips.

"Yes, I guess you're right," she said, leaning back in her chair and resting her walking stick against the arm of it. "He may have even asked us to leave the hotel if he knew what else has taken place with our group so far. What do you think is going on, Lance?"

"I don't know, but I am sure that you'll get to the bottom of this, Sherlock," he said, a big grin on his face. "Let's go find the others and see what they've decided to do for today."

* * *

"There you two are. Come on over," Frank yelled to Lance and Stormy as the two of them walked into the café. "Did you get your breakfast, Stormy? It's mighty good this morning."

"Yes, I did," Stormy said, sitting down in the chair Lance had pulled out from the table for her. She leaned her stick against the table in front of her, steadying it on the floor between her two feet. "Thank you for asking. It was very good indeed."

"So what have you all decided to do for today?" Lance said, sitting down at the table in the chair next to Stormy.

"Well, we've been discussing several of the options we have for today," Clint told them. "First, there is the Lady Bird Johnson Wildflower Center. You can't visit the Austin area without seeing this wonderful place. Another great place to visit is the Art Museum. These are both fine places to see today. Also, we must go and see the Treaty Oak."

"What is the Treaty Oak?" asked Kim, setting her empty glass down.

"It's a huge oak that's at least 500 to 600 years old and has a very fascinating history to it," Clint said. "Tomorrow we will tour the State Capital building in the morning. Does anyone have any preferences about the order for today?"

"I think it might be best to go and see the Wildflower Center this morning while it's a little cooler and then maybe onto the Museum and the old oak," Stormy piped up. "Does that sound good to the rest of you?"

The others in the group agreed with Stormy about the itinerary, all except Tom, who didn't say a thing one way or the other. They all arose from the tables and left the café to prepare for the days events.

Chapter Seventeen

The group was ready and on their way within half an hour. After a pleasant drive, they reached their destination and disembarked from the van in front of the Wildflower Center's entrance. They found themselves surrounded by large spreading oak trees and colorful flower planters where a variety of birds and butterflies hung about. In front of them stood a huge cistern filled with thousands of gallons of collected rain water.

In reading the signs, they found that Lady Bird Johnson, former President Johnson's wife, along with actress Helen Hayes, founded the center in the 1980's. The cistern was built with dark jagged stones on the bottom and then lighter fine cut ones above that. The roof overhead was made of corrugated tin. They learned that water conservation was very important to the center's livelihood.

As Stormy and Lance continued to read about the center's vision to preserve and restore the natural beauty and native plants of the area, and the country for that matter, and to live with them rather than try to conquer or replace them, they were very impressed. They learned that the center was also built to educate the public on how to conserve and landscape with these things, and to instill a love in human kind for the natural things around us.

As they stepped past this area, they noticed magnificent bright red salvia plants near a sign announcing the 'Rockefeller Garden'. Nearby that, was a lovely evergreen mountain laurel. Continuing on their way, the group passed through garden after garden of the most beautiful wild plant specimens any of them had ever seen.

"This place is absolutely fascinating," Stormy said to Lance as they stopped to look at a group of Kindlingweed, or broom snakeweed, with its tiny yellow clusters of flowers gathered at the end of light green branches. "I am glad we got to come and visit here today."

"It's definitely a place well worth the visit," Lance replied, snapping a close up of the Kindlingweed.

"Truly astounding," Amy said, admiring a bunch of deep orange flowers.

"Why don't I take your picture near those pretty flowers, Amy," Lance suggested. "And if you two lovely ladies would like, I will get yours, also. I can send you copies later," he said to Kim and Kati.

"That would be great," Amy said.

"We'd love to have our picture taken here," the sisters agreed. "Use our camera, too, if you will."

Lance took a few shots of Amy, then of the two sisters in the garden. He continued to take a shot or two here and there throughout the garden of the entire group, as well.

The Austin Fires

"That is a good idea to take the pictures here in the gardens," Stormy said to Lance, when she had him alone for a few moments. "They seem to be quite willing to have their pictures taken in a setting like this and don't ask questions about it."

"No, I thought they wouldn't," Lance said. "You should have plenty of photos to choose from for your "lists", my dear."

"Thanks alot, Lance," Stormy said, giving his arm a squeeze as they walked onto the next garden.

After visiting several more areas, they were busily engaged in an exhibit, when they heard a scream coming from up ahead of them. They couldn't see who had screamed as several large shrubs blocked their view. The two of them hurried ahead to see if they could help.

"Kill it, kill it," a lady with a small child was yelling, pointing down to a movement in the flowers not far from her.

"It's okay lady, calm down," Frank was shouting back at her, Nancy leaning on her crutch a ways behind him.

"What's the problem here?" Lance said, arriving beside Frank. "Is someone hurt?"

"No, it's just a snake," Frank shouted, "and this lady has gone into hysterics."

"It's a snake and it tried to kill my child," the woman screamed. "Kill it, please."

Lance went over to the area where the frantic woman was pointing. He carefully looked through the plants along the trail until he saw the creature she was carrying on about.

"There's nothing to worry about, Miss," Lance calmly told her. "This is just a simple garden snake. It won't harm you or your child and at the rate it's retreating, I think it's more afraid of you than you are of it."

The woman calmed down, but still held tightly to the confused child by her side.

Just then a woman dressed in jeans and a t-shirt, with the center's logo written across the front of it, came up to them to see what all the commotion was about. Lance and Frank explained what had happened with the harmless snake. The center's official talked with the frightened woman as the two of them walked away from the area, with the young child in tow.

"Some people leap before they look," Amy said, watching them leave.

"When it has to do with a snake, it's wise to be cautious," Tom said, coming to stand near Amy.

"That's for sure." Frank said, helping Nancy to a nearby bench to rest for a few moments. "Ya'll go on. I think Nancy needs to rest her leg for a spell. We'll catch up with you later."

"Okay, that's a good idea," Stormy said.

The group continued to enjoy their morning, going from garden to garden throughout the center. They learned alot about conservation and many of them decided that they would like to learn more about landscaping with natural plants and shrubs around their own homes.

"This would be a great way to landscape that area of your yard you're not sure what to do with," Kati said to Kim, looking at the display in front of them. "With all of the heavy drought we've been having in Colorado these past few years, it would really save on the water, too."

"I'll look into it when we return home," an excited Kim said, studying the exhibit more closely.

The Austin Fires

After the group had seen the whole main area of the center, they decided to have lunch at the center's café.

"I wonder what is keeping Nancy and Frank?" Stormy said to Lance, looking around her.

"There they are," he replied, pointing down the path behind them.

Stormy turned in time to see a small electric cart pulling up behind her. It came to a stop and the driver jumped out from behind the wheel. He walked around to the other side and helped Nancy out, followed by Frank. They thanked the man, who nodded and got back into the cart and drove it away.

"We were just wondering where you two had gotten to," Lance said as Frank helped Nancy walk to where the group was standing.

"Well, after Nancy was rested up a bit," Frank explained, a little flushed in the face, "we decided to have a look at the rest of the gardens."

"We kind of lost our way," Nancy chimed in, "and if it wouldn't have been for that nice man coming along with his cart, we'd still be out there somewhere." She gestured with her hand across the wide expanse of the gardens.

"Didn't you get a map when you came in," Clint asked, upon hearing Nancy's comments as he joined them. "Everyone was supposed to have one. I'd better have a talk with the manager here about this." As he turned to leave, Frank stopped him.

"We did, but I must have dropped it some where along the way," he said to Clint, smiling. "It wasn't the center's fault, just this old man's."

"Okay," Clint replied, "I'm glad you're okay."

"Things couldn't be better," Frank said, looking over at Nancy. She nodded back at him.

The group headed off to lunch. After they had finished, everyone agreed that the food had been absolutely delicious. They piled back into the van and headed off to their next destination.

* * *

They arrived at the art museum just as a group of noisy teenagers were getting out of a large white van. A tall, lanky teenage boy knocked the hat off of the boys' head who was walking next to him, inviting a sharp reprimand from their teacher.

"Great," Tom mumbled, watching the teenagers and their teacher as they entered the building's front entrance.

"Many of the schools around Austin come here to participate in the art lessons," Clint said. "But don't worry. They'll be in a different area on the grounds."

The art museum was housed in an old early 1900's villa surrounded by lush green lawns and tall, well cared for palm trees and planters.

"I'd love to live in a place like this," Amy said, admiring the exterior of the villa. "Maybe that will be possible some day."

"Maybe," Tom said, looking the place over. "It all depends."

The group entered through the villas' doors and began the tour of its many rooms and exhibits. The art work they saw ranged from old muted colored paintings of buildings and seascapes to wild abstract paintings in various shapes and vivid bright colors. They walked through rooms of

The Austin Fires

exquisite sculptures and displays of ancient earthenware. A large piece of wood was on display from the famous 'Alamo', - the Alamo that history books had written about and that movies were made about.

"Wasn't Daniel Boone present there when the Mexican army attacked and killed most of the soldiers and volunteers at the Alamo?" Nancy asked the museum guide.

"No," he answered, "that is a common mistake. Daniel Boone wasn't at the Alamo. The ones that were there that you hear most about were Davy Crockett and Jim Bowie. There were many other brave men involved in the fight as well. It was in March of 1836 that this group of about 200 men defended the Alamo. It was at dawn on the sixth day of the month that a group of Mexican soldiers attacked them. They fought off the Mexican troops with cannons and small fire arms, but after a second attack, the Mexican soldiers were able to over run the Alamo and prevail against the brave Texans."

"We'll have to go and visit the Alamo some day," Stormy said to Lance after the tour moved on to the next exhibit.

"I'd like that," Lance said. "We'll plan a trip around that some time, but by ourselves. And I think we'll rent a car to tour around in when we go."

"That sounds like fun," she said, following Amy through a door to the next room.

The group continued from room to room, enjoying the museum guide's monologue at each exhibit they came to. As the afternoon progressed, Stormy couldn't shake the feeling that someone was shadowing their moves about the museum, watching them from a distance. Purposely falling back from the group a time or two, she hoped she might discover who it was following them, if anyone at all.

After all, this is a museum, Stormy thought, *and others may innocently be behind us touring the place, also.*

Though she tried to spot anyone that might have been there, she did not see a single soul behind them. It bothered Stormy that she continued to feel a presence behind them all throughout the rest of the museum.

At the end of the tour, the group thanked the museum guide and followed Clint out to look over the museum gardens behind the buildings. It was a lovely spot, over looking a lake of tranquil blue water. The group sat down on the various benches placed through out the garden to rest for a spell.

Chapter Eighteen

"Lance," Stormy quietly said to her husband sitting beside her on the bench, "you will probably think this is a strange question, but did you see anyone else with us as we toured the museum? Like someone following behind us, maybe?"

"Well, considering all that has happened to us so far, I don't think that question is a bit odd," he said, a serious look on his face. "In fact, I thought I felt something myself a time or two, but when I looked around I found no one else in the room with us. Maybe it was just the resident ghost watching from the eyes of the nearby paintings."

"That's it!" Stormy exclaimed.

"What, the museum ghosts?" Lance questioned, leaning forward on the bench.

"No silly, the paintings," she replied in a whisper. "I've read that many museums and art galleries hang special paintings on their walls that have built in cameras to watch the rooms in case of those occasional visitors that are less than honest, not to mention professional thieves. In the past, before the age of electronics, the eyes of paintings would be cut out and made into sliding panels. An observer standing behind the wall could quietly look out and check on suspicious characters. Maybe this museum has a system like this."

"Well, maybe it might have one," Lance replied, "and that might be what we felt."

"Come on," Stormy said, pulling him up from the bench. "I need to find the ladies rest room. It must be back on one of the floors of the museum. Let's go back in and check."

"I think I saw one as we toured through the rooms, come to think of it," Lance said, grinning.

After excusing themselves and telling Clint that they would be right back, Stormy and Lance hurried back to the museum doors before any of the others decided that they, too, might need to use the facilities.

Entering through the same doors the group had exited a short time before, the two of them made their way through the many exhibits as if in search of the restrooms. After looking around for a few minutes, they found a sign directing them in the right direction. They turned and headed down a narrow corridor, arriving at the restrooms. They discovered that another hallway continued past them off to one side.

"Come on," Stormy said in a bare whisper of a voice. "This might be what we are looking for."

Lance followed her down this second hallway which led them to two more doorways. One was marked 'Office', while the other read 'Private". Stormy tried the door marked 'Private' and was pleased to find that its knob turned easily in her hand. She quietly pulled the door open and the two of them slipped quickly through the opening, softly pulling it shut behind them.

Inside, it was pitch dark. Stormy felt along the wall for a light switch, but found none. Reaching inside of her purse, she located her small flashlight and withdrawing it, switched it on. The beam from the light revealed to them another narrow corridor, plus a set of wooden stairs leading upward.

Pointing down the narrow passageway, and getting a nod from Lance, Stormy turned in that direction and slowly proceeded forward. Due to the halls narrowness, they had to walk one in front of the other. Lance would rather have taken the lead, but there wasn't enough room to change places with her.

They slowly crept along the passage, carefully looking at the walls as they went. Down a ways, Lance spotted wires along the top of the wall running along the ceiling in the beam coming from Stormy's flashlight. He grabbed her arm and pulled her to a stop, pointing this out.

"These look like electrical wires" he whispered close to Stormy's ear. "It's hard to say if they run to cameras or are just for the lighting in the museum."

The two continued on, coming to a turn in the passageway. They carefully proceeded around the corner and followed it along. A few yards down the wall, Stormy came to a sudden stop. She put her hand up to the wall and slowly moved it across the wall's rough surface.

"Look at this," Stormy whispered to Lance. "I think we have some kind of lever here. It seems to be stuck though and it won't budge for me. See if you can slide it over."

Stormy made space for Lance and he reached over, feeling the surface of the wall. His hand hit the lever and he tugged at it, applying pressure until it moved a small amount. With a little more pressure, he got the lever to move a few more inches until it came to a stop against a solid wooden board. Stormy leaned over and examined the wall, discovering two small holes about two and a half inches apart in width. Putting her eyes up to the holes, she peered through them.

Stormy could see a room filled with many objects. It took her a few moments to realize that this was one of the rooms where she and her group had been looking at the various displays earlier. In fact, she and Lance had been standing not very far from this wall as they listened to the museum guide tell about one of the nearby displays. No wonder she'd felt like someone was standing behind her, even though she couldn't see anyone.

Stormy moved away from the small holes and motioned for Lance to take a look. Lance moved a step forward, and bending down, looked through the same two holes.

"Interesting," he whispered to Stormy. "I wonder how many more of these there are around the museum."

"Let's have a look along these walls and see what we can find," Stormy whispered back, motioning to Lance as she continued along the wall.

Finding several more of these levers attached to panels, they slid them over, each revealing two small eyeholes behind them. The holes were all about the same height in the walls from the floor where they discovered them. They found though, as Lance tried to move each lever,

The Austin Fires

that most of them were very hard to move and that only of few of them moved aside with ease.

Underneath one of the panels, Lance bent over and picked up an object from off of the floor. Looking it over, he rolled it up and stuffed it into a pant's pocket.

Stormy was looking out of a pair of eyeholes when two women entered the room into which she was peering from behind the wall. She recognized the two sisters, Kim and Kati, as they slowly looked over the room. Stormy motioned for Lance to hold still and put a finger to her lips to caution him to be silent. Continuing to look through the eyeholes in the wall, she observed Kim walk over to one of the displays and proceed to pick up a sword from off of the table it was lying upon. She held it over her head and swung it around and around as if she were attacking, then blocking against an imaginary opponent.

"Put that thing down before someone sees you with it," Kati said, walking up behind her and ducking to one side, barely dodging the sword's blade as it came down close to one of her shoulders. "Watch out, you almost sliced off my arm."

"I wouldn't have hit you with it," Kim said, placing the sword back down on the display table. "I know how to handle a sword, as you know."

"Let's get out of here and find the bathroom," Kati said, turning around and heading toward the opposite doorway. Kim turned and followed behind her sister.

"We'd better get out of here and back to the restrooms before the girls see us coming out of a different door and wonder where we've been," Stormy quietly said to Lance.

He nodded and turning around, headed back in the direction they had come.

Reaching the stairs that led upward, Lance paused at the door from which they had entered the narrow corridor. Stormy switched off her flashlight and put it back into her purse. Lance slowly opened the door and checked to see if anyone was around. Not seeing anyone, he motioned for Stormy to follow him and they stepped through the door and out into the empty corridor. They hurried along the hall and arrived back at the restrooms just as they heard the voices of the two sisters approaching from along the other hallway.

Stormy dashed through the doorway of the women's restroom and hurried into one of the nearby stalls, almost dropping her walking stick as it caught on the stall doors' edge. She pulled it into the stall with her and quickly closed the door as Kim and Kati walked through the restroom doors.

That was a close call, Stormy thought, as the sisters entered the other two stalls in the room. *What we found was a very interesting system. I wonder who made it, and more importantly, who was just using it to spy on our group?*

Once outside the restrooms, Stormy rejoined Lance. She had purposely taken her time washing her hands and combing her hair into place, making sure that Kim and Kati had the opportunity to leave the restroom ahead of her, thus enabling her to have a private talk with Lance.

"I was wondering if you had fallen in or went out a back door," Lance said, his face splitting into a wide grin.

The Austin Fires

"I took my time on purpose so I could talk to you without Kim and Kati joining us for the walk back to the group," Stormy told him, lowering her voice. "That was some passageway we found. What did you think of it?"

"Yes, that was very interesting, indeed," Lance agreed, quietly. "I don't believe that it's used to observe the patrons of the museum on a daily basis. However, I think it's clear that someone used it very recently, most likely today."

"It seems that way, but how can we tell for sure?" she asked him as they walked through the museum toward the side exit doors. The sisters were nowhere in sight.

"I can't be one-hundred percent sure, since most of those levers were very hard to slide over to one side," he said, holding the exit door open for Stormy before exiting through it himself. "If they were used on a regular basis, they would slide more easily, like a few of them did, and be kept in better repair. I did find this on the floor under one of those levers that slid more easily." He reached into his pants pocket and held up his hand, opening it to reveal a candy bar wrapper in it. "As you can see, the chocolate is still wet and sticky."

"That certainly looks fresh to me," she said as he crumbled up the wrapper and stuffed it in back into his pocket. "That being the case, most likely we were being watched from behind that wall as we toured the museum today."

"Yes, I would say so," Lance agreed, "but by whom, and for what reason, is still a mystery."

They arrived back at the group who were still sitting on the garden benches, so there was no more time for further discussions between the two of them.

Chapter Nineteen

They all arose and went back to where the van was parked. The big white bus the teens had arrived in earlier was gone from the parking lot. They got into their van and headed for the next stop, the Treaty Oak Park.

They arrived at the park with great anticipation, exiting the van to join a large group that had gathered around the most magnificent oak tree any of them had ever seen. Clint ushered his group as close to the front of the crowd as he possibly could. A park employee was just beginning to tell the assembled crowd about the history of the old oak tree. The group attentively listened to him.

"The Treaty Oak is an old part of our history here in Austin," the park tour guide began. "It has survived for at least five hundred years through all kinds of weather and catastrophes known to this area of Texas. It originally was one of a group of fourteen large oak trees that the local Indians called the Council Oaks. The Comanche and the Tonkowas used in as a temple of worship. These tribes would meet here under the giant oaks and dance, sing war songs, and hold celebrations and religious ceremonies. Other Indian tribes would brew a mixture of honey and the acorns from these oak trees and give to their braves to drink to safely bring them back from battle."

"It's too bad we couldn't give some of that mixture to our own soldiers before they go over seas to war," Frank said aloud. "We might see many more of them return to their waiting loved ones."

Several of the crowd around him nodded and readily agreed to his comments.

"An interesting part of local history, and the reason for this tree being called the 'Treaty Oak', comes from a legend that tells of Stephen F. Austin signing the first boundary treaty with the local Indians under this oak tree. This treaty was called for as several people, including children, were killed by the Indians for coming too close to these trees," the park guide continued. "Later, in the 1900's, after all the other oaks in this group had been cut down for one reason or another, and this last tree's piece of land was up for sale, the people of Texas fought back to spare this last oak. There were rights movements and marches, speeches given and letters written. The land and this tree were finally spared and bought by the city of Austin and is the park you see here today.

"This is a lot of history for one tree to have," Stormy said. "It reminds me of the historic Red Wood trees in that park in Northern California. Those are magnificent trees to behold, as well."

"Yes," Lance said, looking up at the huge oak in front of them. "It's a good thing when people show that they care about the world we live in."

The Austin Fires

"Another, more recent side note of this oaks history," the park guide went on, "is that in 1989 a man who was spurned by his girlfriend massively poisoned this tree and it was almost lost forever. Through the efforts of many it was saved and has even recovered a little over the years since then. In addition, several of the young saplings from its acorns have been sent around the country to carry on its legacy."

The guide finished up his speech and the crowd began milling around the park, a few of them asking further questions of the park guide.

"Come over here," Clint called to the group, motioning them over to a couple of picnic tables a ways from the tree.

As the group neared the tables, several picnic baskets laden down with delicious looking foods set out upon one of the tables caught their attention. There were bottles of sodas and spring water set amongst plastic plates and cups, with utensils spread along side.

"I thought you all might enjoy a picnic here in the park since it is getting so late. Our driver was so kind as to go and pick it up for us. So let's all dig in everyone and enjoy the feast."

"This was a great idea," Stormy said, as she grabbed a plate and began dishing up a large spoon of baked beans.

"I agree whole heartedly, my dear," Lance replied, grabbing a plate and following her lead.

"This is great tasting salad," Stormy said to Lance as she swallowed the last bite of her potato salad. "My mouth says it would like some more of this delightful food, but my stomach says, no way."

"Then I guess we'd both better listen to our stomachs," Lance said, eyeing the plate of cookies not far from his reach, "though mine says it might have room for just one more cookie."

"You might think about the times you've been up late at night with indigestion due to eating one more thing," Stormy said, concerned, "before you pick that cookie up and take a bite."

"I guess you're right about that," Lance said, sighing. "I'll leave room for dessert after our dinner tonight, instead."

"Yes, maybe so," Stormy said, laughing as she hung onto Lance's arm as he helped her up from the picnic table's bench.

"Hey," Kati yelled over to them as they started to walk away from the bench, "Will one of you take our picture over by the Treaty Oak? Please?"

"Sure," Lance said, guiding Stormy by the arm to the spot where the sisters were standing. "Okay, stand together over there in front of that part of the oak. Stand a little bit to the right, Kim, the tree's branch is shading your face too much. Perfect, now smile and say cheese."

As Lance clicked off a third picture of the sisters, Stormy noticed a tree branch behind them move slightly over to one side, remain that way for a few moments, then snap back into place.

That definitely wasn't any animal that I know of, Stormy thought, staring at the spot intently, "*unless they have very talented squirrels in this park. That had to be a human being that moved that branch. Who's hiding in that old tree, and why watch us?*

Having promised Lance she would talk to him first before running off to investigate things, she waited for him to snap the last picture of the sisters in front of the

The Austin Fires

tree and then pulled him aside. She'd been keeping an eye on the branch just in case it moved again.

"Lance," Stormy said quietly, "while you were busy taking pictures of the sisters, I saw a branch move aside and stay there as if someone was watching us. The branch snapped back into place, but then a few minutes later it happened again."

"Are you sure it wasn't an animal like a squirrel or a bird?" Lance asked her, looking over at the old oak tree.

"I'm positive that it only could have been a human," Stormy replied. "It wasn't an action that an animal would do. I waited for you to finish taking the photos of the girls so we could investigate it together. Let's go and check out the tree up closer."

"Good girl," he agreed, "but we'll have to be careful no one sees us that close to the oak. They might not like it and think we're trying to harm the old tree."

Lance held out his arm for Stormy, and taking it, they pretended to stroll slowly around the park, coming nearer the oak tree, and acting as if they were deep in serious conversation.

From time to time, they glanced around keeping an eye on the crowd for just the right moment. When they were sure that no one was looking their way, the two of them darted under the branches of the old oak and made their way to the heart of the tree. They stood very still next to the oaks' trunk, listening intently for any sound that would indicate there was another human within its branches.

They did not have to wait long before they heard what sounded like a person clearing their throat, after which they heard rustling noises coming from the far left side of the tree.

Stormy touched Lance's arm with her one hand and held her other one up to her ear to ask him if he, too, had heard the sounds. Understanding her gesture, he held his own hand to one ear, nodding his head. Putting a finger to his lips for silence, he led the way in the direction of the sounds, carefully picking his way through the oaks' many branches.

As they neared the other side of the tree, they spotted a figure standing a short distance in front of them with its' back turned away from them. The person was peering out through the trees branches at the happenings of the other people in the park beyond.

Lance signaled Stormy to go off to the right side of where the person stood while he would go off to the persons left. She proceeded forward to her assigned spot, stepping as slowly and carefully as she could, Lance doing the same on his side.

Just as they came with in an arms length of the person, Stormy's foot came down on a small twig, breaking it with a loud snap. The startled person jerked its' head around in her direction, revealing a young, brown haired, lightly mustached man of no more than thirty years of age. With a drop of his jaw, he momentarily stared at Stormy, surprised and a little puzzled.

Regaining his wits about him, the man turned and headed toward Stormy. Stepping back a pace or two as he approached her, and unsure of what she should do, she wished that she hadn't left her walking stick back at the picnic table.

Chapter Twenty

The man continued to close the distance between them, but stopped in his tracks as an arm reached around his neck and pulled him backwards.

If the situation hadn't been so serious, Stormy would've burst out laughing from the expression on the man's face as Lance grabbed him tighter, putting him in a neck and back lock. She was sure the man had never been in this compromising position before now. Afraid to move, and unable to do so, the man stood quietly still awaiting their next move.

"Okay, buddy, what's going on here?" Lance said in a deep growling voice. "Why are you hiding in this oak tree spying on everyone around here? You must be the one who's been following us around all day."

Lance loosened his hold slightly on the man's neck, allowing him to answer.

S. A. Slack

Clearing his throat, the man hesitated for a moment and then decided he'd better say something to ease his precarious position.

"Um, I'm doing research on this fine old oak tree and I needed to get some samples, so I climbed in here to take a better look," the man started. "Now that I have finished collecting the things, I, um, need to get back to my studies. I was just deciding how I would leave here with out bothering anyone."

"Okay, so where are these samples you took," Lance asked him, still holding him in a tight grasp. "I don't see any bag or container for you to put them into."

"Um, I was just taking sample notes in my small note book," the man replied nervously. "I have it right here in my front pocket along with my pen."

"What do you think, Storm," Lance asked her, obvious doubt filling his voice. "Do you think we can believe him?"

"I don't know. What's your name?" Stormy asked, coming closer to where the two men stood.

"My name is Marshall, I mean Marston, yeah, Mike Marston," the man said, clearing his throat once more.

"Mr. Marston or Marshall is it? Give it up," Lance said. "Tell us the truth or I'll march you right out of here and turn you over to the park authorities. Around here, they don't take kindly to anyone trying to bring harm to this nice old tree of theirs, or trying to burn down half of the city and its residents either."

"Oh no, I would never harm this wonderful old tree," the man said, obvious distress in his voice. "I've been coming here since I was a small boy and…um," the man stopped talking and looked down at the ground. "Okay,

The Austin Fires

I might as well tell you the truth," he said, lifting his head and looking Stormy straight in the eyes. "I'm a detective for the Austin police force, newly assigned to the arson squad. My identification is in my top left pocket if you'd like to see it."

"Well, we'll just have to take a look at that," Lance said, reaching around and checking in the left pocket of the man's shirt.

He withdrew a small billfold and handed it to Stormy. "Look this over, Storm, and see if this man is really who he claims to be."

Stormy took the billfold, holding it in front of her as she opened it up and examined it closely.

"Well, if this is really your true identification, Mr. Ned Marshall," she announced, "you really are a detective for the Austin police department."

"I guess I had better let you go then, detective," Lance said, releasing the man. "Sorry about that, but we thought you were the nut that has been following our group around and setting fires and such."

"That's okay," Detective Marshall said, rubbing his arms and clearing his throat once again. "I guess I did look a bit suspicious lurking here in this tree, now that I think about it. I guess I'll have to work on that."

"That you should," Stormy agreed with the man. "So, are you actually the one that's been following our group around all this week, hiding in corridors and stairwells?"

"Corridors and stairwells, Mrs. Winters?" the detective said, bewildered. "I don't know what you mean. I was assigned to keep an eye on your group since the night of the football game your group attended at the Longhorn's stadium. Since I have other duties to attend to, I've only been able to watch you from time to time. I just arrived as your group got here for the park guides' lecture."

"Then you're not the only one who's been following us around this week, detective," Lance told him. "Someone else has been following us consistently from place to place as our group has been touring around Austin. They've snuck into our rooms, started fires in the places we've been to, and several other strange things have happened."

"That's why the arson squad has assigned me to this case," Detective Marshall said, placing his badge and billfold back into his shirt pocket. "Your tour group has had too many of these incidents to completely rule them out as accidental. I was to follow you around and see what I could find out about who might be setting these fires. We're concerned that maybe it's someone from your tour group?" He looked questioningly from one to the other of them, hoping for an answer.

"We've been wondering about that ourselves," Stormy answered, "but we've not seen any concrete evidence to support that it is someone from the group that's doing these things. We have seen, however, a mysterious person that we believe it to be a man, shadowing us around as we've already mentioned to you. I think he may believe that I know who he is as he has already locked me in a basement room at the hotel and spooked the carriage we were riding in with another couple from the group. I assume he possibly hoped he might injure one or more of us to get us out of the way."

"This sounds much more serious than we thought it was before, and the fires are a serious enough problem as it is," said Detective Marshall. "I don't want my Captain

The Austin Fires

to know that my cover has been blown on my very first case with the Arson squad, so please do me a favor and do not mention this to anyone. However, I'd like to keep in touch with you," he said, reaching into his right shirt pocket, withdrawing a business-sized card, and handing it to Stormy. "Here's my card with my cell phone number and e-mail address on it. If anything else happens or you find out something new, please don't hesitate to get in touch with me. I'll contact you if I need to ask you any more questions. Do you have a cell phone I can reach you on?"

"Yes, detective, I carry my cell phone with me most of the time," Stormy said.

"Unless she's out sneaking around the hotel in her bathrobe and slippers in the middle of the night," Lance said, grinning over at his wife.

"Ignore him," Stormy said, writing her cell phone number on a piece of paper she had taken from her purse and handing it to the detective. "I just thought I heard a noise late at night and wanted to find out what it was."

"You need to be careful, Mrs. Winters," the detective told her. "You might have a run in with an unsavory character that you might not be able to escape from. Please call me or the hotel's detective if you happen to see or hear anything suspicious from now on."

"Yes," Lance chimed in. "He has a good point there, my dear."

"Right," she said, looking at her husband. "By the way, did you say you were watching us at the football game the other night?"

"Yes, that was my first assignment on this case. I was told to follow you and see what was going on," he replied.

"You didn't happen to be following the two sisters and I in the passageway from the restrooms back to our seats, wearing a Texas Longhorn shirt and blue jeans, did you?" she asked the detective.

"I was that obvious, was I?" he said, chagrinned. "I was hoping you hadn't noticed me that night. I guess I'll have to practice a little more on that one, too."

"My wife is just good at spotting that sort of thing," Lance told him. "Don't worry."

"Well, I don't think it would be wise for us to be seen together, so why don't you leave the tree by the way you entered it," said the detective, pointing a finger, "and I'll wait a few minutes before I leave this way. And be careful not to let anyone see you leaving the tree. They might ask you too many questions." With this he moved away from them and pushed the trees' branches aside to see where the others were.

Lance and Stormy retraced their steps, carefully picking their way to the other side of the oak tree. Looking out through the branches to see if any one was around or looking their way, they slipped out from under the oak and walked arm in arm as if they had just come from a long leisurely walk around the park together.

"What do you think of our young Detective Marshall, Lance," Stormy asked her husband as they walked slowly back to rejoin the rest of their group.

"He seems well enough," Lance replied. "A little bit inexperienced at shadowing his quarry, but he should get better at it given some time with the squad. He seems sincere in trying to find out what's going on though."

"He certainly isn't the one that's been sneaking around all over the place, shadowing our group," she said, as they neared the picnic tables. "That character seems much more shady and better at sneaking around, with intent on doing someone in our group some harm. I hope we can find out who it might be before they strike again."

"Yes, me, too," Lance said, pulling her tighter against him.

"There you two love birds are," Amy said as Lance and Stormy arrived back at the picnic tables arm in arm. "Clint said we're to get our things together and take them back to the van. He and the driver took the baskets to the van a few minutes ago."

"I guess we're right on time then," Lance said, holding out his arm and smiling his most charming smile. "Shall we go, my lady?"

"I believe we shall, my dear," Stormy returned, and the two walked off at a graceful pace.

Chapter Twenty One

The group piled into the van and headed back to the Drakeston. Once there, they began breaking into groups, some heading for the elevator and their rooms to rest and change for the night's activities. Clint had reminded them that they were to meet down at the hotel's pool for a swim and a Texas style barbeque that the hotel was putting on for all of the hotel's guests that evening.

"Before then, you're free to rest, go shopping, or whatever else you would like to do. Just make sure you're back here and at the swimming pool area by 6:30," Clint had said as they had been departing the van.

As they reached the elevators, Stormy told Lance that she wanted to rest and make a few notes before this evenings activities. He thought this would be a good idea for both of them as it had been a long day so far. The sisters joined them and they rode the elevator up to their rooms.

"I bought that new swim suit before we left," Kim said to Kati as they exited the elevator at their floor. "I hope it still fits me after all the food I've been eating since we came on this trip."

"Let's both go try our suits on to make sure they fit," Kati said, turning in the direction of their room. "I have been eating that same delicious food, also, you know. See you guys later."

"Maybe I'd better try my suit on as well," Stormy said to Lance as they entered their room. "Mine might not fit so well either."

Walking over to her suitcase, she opened it to remove her swimming suit.

"Lance, someone's been in our room and has gone through our things."

"How do you know that?" Lance said, stepping out of the bathroom and looking around the room. "It looks like we left it this morning, except that the maid's been in to make the beds and bring us fresh towels and glasses."

"I had left my mystery book on the chair here when we left and now it's in my suitcase," she replied, picking up the book and holding it in her hand. "You might check over your things and see if anything's been moved or taken."

Lance looked through his suitcases, then the dresser drawers where he had placed most of his things. At first he didn't see anything out of place, but on closer inspection, he noticed that a few of his handkerchiefs were bunched up and pushed to the opposite side of the drawer where he had placed them when he had unpacked. Nothing seemed to be missing, though.

The Austin Fires

Going over to his laptop on the desk and seeing that it was still where he had placed it, Lanced opened it up. He tapped a few keys on the keyboard, read several lines of print that showed up on the screen, and then turned to Stormy.

"It looks like someone was definitely trying to access my laptop while we were away, Storm," Lance told her.

"How can you tell?"

"I installed a security program on my laptop when I bought it last year just in case something like this ever happened," he replied. "I guess it finally came in handy this time.'

"What does it tell you?" she asked.

"I put my computer in sleep mode when we left and as you know, this means you have to put a password in when you open it back up to access any of the files on it. This program tells me whenever someone has tried to access my laptop and what passwords they've typed into it to do so," Lance explained. "It's very interesting to see some of the words they tried to use to break into it."

"Like what kinds of words?" Stormy asked, coming over to the table where Lance sat looking at the laptop's screen.

"The first thing they tried is your name 'Stormy' and then the next thing was 'Storm'. How original. Only a moron would be that simple with their passwords," Lance grumbled.

"You worked in computer security for the military, dear," Stormy reminded him, "so you're more aware than most about these things. Not everyone is, you know. What else did they try?"

"It looks like they discovered my birth date and tried that, also, and then they tried yours as well to see if they could break in," Lance said, scanning the characters on the screen in front of him. "Then when that didn't work, they tried 'Phoenix', then 'Arizona', and then a bunch of other unrelated words. They not only seemed to be persistent, but they seem to know a lot about you and I and our personal information."

"I wonder why they were trying so hard to break into your computer," Stormy said, moving around the room looking for anything else out of place. "What could you possibly have on there that would be of such importance or interest to them? In other words, what did they expect to find?"

"Who knows what they were hoping to find," Lance said, "but at least they weren't successful in their attempts to do so."

"A thought just crossed my mind," Stormy said, putting a finger to her lips, "but maybe it's nothing to worry about."

Taking a pen and tablet from the desk drawer and writing out a message on a slip of paper, she held it up for Lance to read. It said "Let's check the room and see if anyone has bugged it."

Lance raised an eyebrow at the suggestion, but nodded in agreement. They carried on a light conversation about trivial things as they did a through search of the entire room, including the bathroom and closet.

Finding no such devices of any kind hiding any where in the room, Stormy flopped down on the bed with a sigh.

The Austin Fires

"I know you must think that was a silly thing for us to do, but under the circumstances I just thought we might as well check and see if there were any bugs around the room. I feel better now that we've looked."

"No, that's a good thing to think of, and it didn't hurt to check just in case." Lance flopped down onto the bed beside her. "We just want to be careful, but not become paranoid."

"I don't think being extra careful is the same thing as being paranoid," she explained. "We just have to keep our eyes open, that's all."

"Let's have a look at your lists," Lance said, putting his password into the laptop and opening up a file. "Take out your small notebook and we'll add the new notes you've taken since putting the others here in your folder."

Stormy opened her purse and withdrew her notebook. Flipping it open, she turned to her latest notes and read them aloud to Lance. His fingers flew over the keys as he added the latest items to files and placed the information under the headings of the various members in their tour group that were pertinent to each of the individuals. This completed, he and Stormy, who had come to sit by him in another chair at the desk, went over each of the members in their group, one by one.

"Why don't we start with what we have learned about Frank so far," Stormy suggested. "Then we'll go on to Nancy afterwards and so on. It'll be like they do in the movies when they want to decide who done it."

"Okay, my dear, Frank it is," Lance agreed, bringing up his file.

Frank's picture flashed onto the screen in front of them.

"Here's what we have so far on Frank. We know he's in his mid-seventies and married to Nancy. He loves anything to do with trains, from real ones to model ones, and he's in the process of building a miniature city in his house for his trains. He says he's retired from the rail road, but he was forced to do so."

"He seems bitter at the railroad, or someone who works there for forcing him to retire and for substituting a younger man in his place," Stormy put in. "That could be a reason to hold a grudge against someone and maybe even take revenge."

"That's true," Lance agreed. "Don't forget what Nancy said about the man Frank had gotten fired for being lazy and not doing his job. I'm sure that the man was not too fond of Frank after he did that."

"No, probably not," she agreed. "Frank also talks very loudly indicating that after all those years of running a noisy train engine up and down the tracks it seems to have left him a little deaf. Now let's look over the list of any incidents he's been involved in so far on this tour, which we know of that is."

"Well, so far as we know," Lance said, clicking and bringing up the information concerning Frank, "these are the things we have listed for him. First, he was on the bus when it caught fire, though we were all riding on that. Next, he was on the wild carriage ride with you and me. In addition, his wife, Nancy, was knocked down at the university and had her purse stolen from her, and then he was the one to complain to Clint about this tour not being very safe. It's interesting that we've not heard any complaints from the others about this so far."

The Austin Fires

"Yes, you're right," Stormy agreed. "Now let's look at what we have so far on Nancy."

"Nancy's file, coming up at once, detective," Lance said, clicking the mouse button a few times. "Here's the file on her."

"Thanks, Watson," "Let's see what we have here. She's also in her mid-seventies, married to Frank of course, though they've not said for how long, and she owns and runs a small craft store in her town," she said, reading from the list. "She's not said what she did before she bought the store though. She seems quieter and more on the meeker side than her husband is, but a few times on this trip, by the comments I've heard her say to her husband, I don't think she's as meek and quiet as she appears to be."

"Yes, many times first appearances can be deceiving, that's for sure," Lance remarked, scrolling down Nancy's file to see what she had been involved in so far. "Okay, Nancy was in the bus fire with us, and on the wild carriage ride, too. She even lost her crutch in the street during that ride. And before that, she was knocked down at the university and her large tapestry bag was stolen."

"Yes, and she seemed very attached to that bag of hers," Stormy said. "She made a strange comment to me that I didn't know the half of it when I told her I was sorry her purse was stolen."

"I wonder what she had in that purse that was so special to her," Lance said. "She didn't want anyone else to see whatever she had, did she."

"Makes one wonder doesn't it," she said. "Is that all we have on her so far?"

"Yes, I think so," he replied. "Who do you want to look at next?"

"I think we should look over what we have in Kim and Kati's files next," Stormy said, pulling her chair closer to the table in order to see the laptop screen better.

"Okay, we'll look at Kim first," Lance said. "This is a nice photo of her. These two sisters look a lot like each other, don't they. Kim's the older of the two sisters and both are from Colorado Springs, Colorado. She's in her forties, and her last child just graduated from high school and went off to college, leaving her free to travel. It's too bad that neither of the sisters' husbands could join them on the tour."

"Yes, it's a shame," Stormy said, kissing Lance lightly on the cheek. "I'm glad you could come along, as I wouldn't have wanted to be on this trip without you. Now what else do we have about her?'

"She runs a computer graphics company there in the Springs with her sister, Kati," Lance told her. "I heard that she took over someone's company in which she had been an employee for a few years before that. Kim said that the previous owner was upset with the price that Kim had bought it for and said Kim got it for a steal."

"Where did you hear that from?" she asked him, surprised.

"Oh, in the museum before the fire broke out," Lance said, "Kati was telling me all about their business while Kim was away getting a drink of water or something. Kati even told me that Kim insisted that Kati work the company with her from the start as partners."

"That's very interesting news," Stormy said. "Please make sure you make a note of this in both Kim and Kati's

The Austin Fires

files. It might fit into this puzzle somewhere. Now, let us see what else we know. Kim fell that night at the ninety-nine steps and went sliding down the hill in all that mud. Do you think someone could've pushed her down?"

"Anything could've happened," he replied. "It was raining so hard I couldn't see a thing. Too bad they hadn't asked us to take a picture of them then. We might've caught her fall on film and then we would know for sure. Maybe we could look at all those other pictures we took for them in case there are other clues about something else on them."

"Good idea," she said, "we should do that as soon as we have time. I think another interesting thing about Kim is what she did at the museum today. Remember when we were behind the wall looking out, and the two sisters came into the room into which we were peering? Thinking no one was watching, Kim picked up that sword and swung it around like a pro. She as much as said she was when her sister told her to put it down."

"That's something we'll have to write down in her file in case it comes up again," Lance said, adding it to Kim's file. "And I think we should add something else that Kati told me. She said that Kim's husband works for a pharmaceutical company." He keyed in the information and turned to Stormy. "Okay, done. Now I guess it will be Katie's file, right?"

"Right," she agreed. "She has some of the same things, of course, in her file as does Kim. Such as, she's in her forties, no children left at home, and she works with her sister at the computer graphics design company. But it seems to me that she is a little more mysterious in some ways than Kim is."

"How's that?" Lance asked.

"Well, at the bus fire while we were waiting for the fire engines to arrive," she said, "I saw her look around and then try to carry off someone else's suitcase from the pile. I saw her sister motion for her to drop it and she did."

"I wonder who's luggage she was trying to walk off with and why?" Lance said. "That does seem a bit odd to me, too. Oh, and Kati also told me that her youngest son, the one that just went off to college, loves anything to do with trains. He would feel right at home with Frank."

"Yes, I would think so. And what about when we were at the History Museum and she asked us if we knew that couple in Phoenix," Stormy said. "When we said we didn't, she quickly brushed it off and said she had to get back to her sister. And then later, she and Kim came out of the bathroom laughing, when only moments before Amy came out crying. That was strange."

"Yes, it is. Okay, how about looking at Tom next?" Lance said, pulling up his photo and file.

"That would be next on the list I think," Stormy said. "He sure seems to be a rather moody sort of guy, scowling most of the time and looking glum. As we know, he's in his late twenties, is engaged to Amy, and is a medical student at the University of California at Los Angeles. Amy told me that his father, a doctor in family practice, is pushing him very hard to be tops in all of his classes and that the stress of this is getting to Tom. She also made an interesting comment about how Tom's father had his medical practice there in Los Angeles up until about six months ago. There had been a major lawsuit against him, something to do with a man's wife dying due to Tom's dad misdiagnosing the wife and giving her the wrong

The Austin Fires

medication. He was found not at fault, but moved his practice to San Diego instead."

"There was probably too much publicity about the case and it hurt his practice in L.A.," Lance guessed. "What else do we have? Ah, I see that you wrote down that Tom was no where to be seen when that fire took place in the museum, then he appeared out of no where behind you. I wonder where he was?"

"And remember when we were out on the balcony and I saw him down in the street handing that man something which he stuffed into his pocket," Stormy reminded him. "I wonder what was up with that?"

"I don't know," Lance said. "Is there any more to put into his file?"

"No, not at the moment, so I guess that leaves Amy. Let's look at what we have in her file."

"Well, as we already said, she is engaged to Tom, is an Art major at UCLA, and is also in her late twenties," Lance read, having pulled up her file. "She appears to come from a wealthy family. She hardly eats any food, at least that I've seen here on the tour, no matter where we dine. Maybe she snacks a lot at night," he grinned.

"Maybe," Stormy laughed, "but I doubt it. I wouldn't mind having her figure."

"I think you are lovely the way you are," he replied, kissing her gently.

"Thank you, dear," she beamed, "but we must not get side tracked right now. Did we write down in her file when I saw her come from the bathroom in tears that day at the museum?"

"Yes, it's right here. I wonder what she was so upset about."

"I think I might know why," Stormy said, "but I'll wait and watch some more before I say anything just yet. Then Amy is pushed over board, and…"

"Wait," Lance said, holding up his hand as he looked more closely at the computer screen. "You forgot to put that in her file on here. Let me add that for you."

"I did forget, didn't I," Stormy said, leaning closer to the screen as Lance typed. "I'm glad you caught that. Thanks for adding it in. Tom sure seemed to make light of Amy possibly being pushed in."

"Do you remember what you told me he said?" Lance asked. "That he knew she was a good swimmer. I don't think he was all that worried about it."

"Well, he seemed to act the same way when someone broke into Amy's room and we told him about the foot we saw going out of the window," Stormy said. "Actually, Amy didn't seem that concerned when we told her about it either, come to think of it. She even refused to call security, remember?"

"Yes, I do," Lance said, scanning down the file. "What else do we have down for her?"

"That's all I can think of for now," she answered. "But wait, what about our tour guide, Clint? Maybe we should list a few things about him, as well. Like how he seems to disappear a lot of the time when we visit places, telling us he's getting reservations or planning for something. Don't you think that he would've taken care of those things in advance of the tour?"

"I would think so," Lance replied, "but maybe he does things differently. We'll fill out a file for him if you want to, but there's not a lot to list for him. I guess we could jot down what the brochure said about him that

The Austin Fires

came in our packet with the tickets and paper work before the tour. I remember it said that he's only been with the company for about six months now and that he'd come from another tour company before that. I wonder why he changed companies any way? I wonder if he had some sort of falling out with the previous company or he just didn't like their policies."

"Yes, I've wondered about that, too. Oh, look at the time. I guess we'd better get into our swim suits and head down to the barbeque. They should be about to start the festivities."

"You're right," Lance said, looking at his watch. "Let's go get us some of that good Texas barbeque."

Chapter Twenty-Two

Lance and Stormy left their room and headed for the elevator. On the way down, Lance asked her if she had any more thoughts as to what was going on with this tour group. "I just don't see how any of it fits together," he said, a thoughtful look on his face.

"I was thinking about all of the things we've written down for each person on this tour as I changed for into my suit," she said, "and a few ideas came to me. I'm strongly beginning to wonder about certain things, but let me think on them for a while and I'll let you know later."

"Okay, here we are any way," he said as the elevator doors opened. He stepped back to let Stormy exit first. "Let's go to the pool area and I'll help you watch the others some more, while we eat, of course."

"Of course."

Many of the hotel's guests were milling around the pool, seeming to be enjoying themselves. Others were lazily swimming in the cool water, while still others were playing water volley ball at the far end of the pool. Several people were sitting around the tables enjoying the food as they chatted away with friends and acquaintances.

Lance and Stormy got in the line for food, filling their plates full of a variety of wonderful looking items. They spotted Frank waving them over to where he and Nancy were sitting and decided to join them.

"Hi," Frank said, in his usual loud voice. "I was hoping we'd see you here. We'd be happy to have you sit with us at our table here."

"We'd love to sit with you," Stormy said, politely reaching for a chair. She wasn't sure that Lance was too overjoyed about sitting with them, but she knew he would be polite all the same. "Hi, Nancy, how's the food?"

"It's great!" Frank bellowed, answering for his wife. "Wait until you taste these ribs. They're to die for."

"I hope not," Lance whispered to Stormy as he picked up a rib from off of the plate in front of him. After taking a bite, he had to agree that they were some of the best he'd ever eaten.

"I really like the food they serve here in Texas," Nancy said. "A lot of it has a rich spicy taste to it, more than the foods we eat back home. Frank and I were talking about picking up some of the spices and barbeque sauces they have here, so we could use them at home."

"It would be like bringing a little Texas flavor home with us," Frank cried out, making several heads turn in their direction.

I wonder how Nancy puts up with his loud voice, Stormy thought, *but I guess she's gotten used to it over the years. I don't know if I could do so.*

The Austin Fires

As they were enjoying the food, a uniformed police officer made his way along the pool's edge and through the crowd. He approached their table and stopped beside Nancy.

"Good evening, folks," he said, tipping the brim of his gray Stetson to the women. "I'm sorry to disturb you at dinner time, but I believe I have something that belongs to one of you ladies. The Sergeant asked me to return this to you, ma'am."

The officer set the large paper bag he'd been carrying on the table and reached inside of it. He pulled out the large tapestry bag belonging to Nancy.

"Oh, Frank!" Nancy shouted out. "They've found my bag. Thank you so very much officer, and thank your sergeant for me, too."

She grabbed the tapestry bag from the officer's outstretched hands and held it tightly to her chest, causing Stormy and Lance to exchange questioning glances.

"What about the man who attacked my wife and knocked her down?" Frank bellowed, rising to his feet. "Did you find any fingerprints on the bag? Did you catch the scumbag and lock him up?

"Calm down, sir," the police officer said. "We're still looking for him. As for any prints, he must have worn gloves. We couldn't find any other fingerprints on the bag except those of your wife's, which we matched to the samples she gave us the other day. It looks like he went through your wife's bag and then tossed it beside one of the old buildings on campus. We need you, Mrs. Thornton" he said, turning toward Nancy, "to take a look in your bag, please, and see if anything is missing."

Nancy placed the large tapestry bag down on the table and began searching through its contents. After a minute or two, she sighed and looked up at the officer.

"All that seems to be missing is the extra money I had tucked into an inside pocket," she said. "It was a twenty dollar bill that I keep in my bag for emergencies. I guess the man had an emergency he needed it for. Every thing else seems to be here, officer."

"Okay," the officer said, writing down the missing money in his small note book, "but if you find that something else is missing that you didn't notice right now, or have any questions for us, call me at this number as soon as you can." Withdrawing a business card from his shirt pocket, he handed it to Nancy. "We'll be in touch with you as soon as we find the guy who did this. Have a good day folks." He tipped the brim of his hat once more and left, heading back the way he had come.

"Wow," Stormy said, looking at the bag Nancy was holding. "You rarely get your things back when they're stolen from you. You were very lucky that you only had twenty dollars in your purse, and that's all he took."

"Yes," Lance agreed, "it's definitely exceptional to get your purse or anything else back, once it's been taken."

"I'm sure glad you have your bag, dear," Frank said, looking at the bag on the table in front of his wife, "It'd be a shame if you lost your award after all you went through to win and keep the thing."

"What award is that?" Stormy asked. "What was it for?"

"She took the title for first place this year at our county fair for the wonderful sweaters and slippers she knits," Frank spoke up when Nancy hesitated to answer. "The

The Austin Fires

woman she stole the best knitting title from at the fair had held it for the last ten years for her knitting expertise. That woman was quite livid over Nancy's taking the title away from her and said some rather nasty stuff about Nancy and her knitting needles. She was a very poor loser and even went so far as to try and have the judges disqualify Nancy and her knitting."

"That's a terrible thing to do," Stormy said. "You're right, that woman was a poor loser indeed. Would it be okay if we took a look at your award, Nancy?"

"Yes, show it to them, Nancy," Frank bellowed out, "You've earned it fair and square."

Nancy opened her bag and reached inside. She pulled forth a wooden plaque with a bright blue ribbon attached to it. As she went to hand it over, Stormy noticed that some strands of yarn were stuck to the edge of the plaque. Nancy saw them too and stopped to remove the yarn before any more of it was pulled from out of her bag.

"I brought several skeins of yarn with me in case I had time to knit another sweater or two for my shop," Nancy said. "I guess it got caught on the corner of my award. Wait just a moment while I untangle it."

As they waited for Nancy to unravel the strands, Stormy noticed something shiny caught in one of the pieces of yarn. It looked vaguely familiar, and she leaned forward to get a better look. As she did so, Kim and Kati walked up to the table.

"Great!" Kati said. "I see you got your bag back. I hope they found that thief and locked him up."

"They haven't found him yet," Frank said, disgustedly. "They had better soon though before he strikes again. Thieves don't do this kind of thing only once, you know.

They'll hit some other poor woman and steal her purse or rob a curb store next time and kill someone."

"You're right," Lance said. "They usually keep on robbing people until they get caught."

"What's that hanging from that piece of yarn, Nancy?" Stormy asked, leaning even closer to look at the object.

"What? Oh, I'm not sure," Nancy said, untangling the object from out of the yarn. "It looks like an earring in the shape of a seahorse, I believe. I wonder what it's doing in here."

"It's a pretty earring. Is it yours, Nancy?" Stormy asked, studying Nancy's face.

"No," Nancy replied, puzzled. "It's not mine. I've never seen this earring before in my life."

"May I see it?" Stormy asked.

Nancy handed it to her and Stormy placed it in the palm of her hand where Lance could also look at it.

Looking at it up close, they saw that it was definitely a seahorse shaped earring and that it had a small blue sapphire placed in it for an eye. Stormy was sure that it was identical to the one they had found at the history museum on the floor where the fire had taken place.

"Are you sure this is not your earring?" Lance asked Nancy.

"I already told you that I have never seen it before," Nancy said, anger creeping into her voice.

"What's this all about?" Frank roared. "Why are you asking Nancy about this little earring? Have you seen it some where before?"

"Well, one like it," Stormy said. "There was an earring that was identical to this one that was found lying by that

The Austin Fires

can that started on fire at the history museum the other day."

"Well, it wasn't my wife's," Frank said, defending Nancy. "I'm sure of that."

"It probably got into your bag by mistake," Stormy said. "Don't worry about it. But you might check with the museum and see if it matches the one they're holding onto. Maybe the same guy was at the museum who knocked you down and took your purse."

"Maybe," Kati said, looking closer at the earring. "It kind of looks like..."

"Come on, Kati," Kim said, interrupting her sister. "We have to be going, right now." Kim pulled on Kati's arm and led her away, a panicky look crossing her face. "We have an appointment to keep. Bye all."

Kim hurried away with a puzzled Kati in tow. They soon disappeared into the crowd of hotel guests.

"I wonder where they're going in such a hurry,' Lance asked Stormy. "It must be an important appointment she doesn't want to miss."

"I guess so," Stormy said thoughtfully, "but I wonder."

The four of them finished their meal and continued a lively conversation with Frank telling them of his many adventures on the railroad. After a while, when Frank and Nancy went to pick out a dessert from the dessert bar, Lance suggested that they go for a swim in the pool.

"It sounds like fun to me," Stormy said. Getting to her feet, she said "Last one in is a rotten egg." With that, she hurried off in the direction of the pool.

Lance slowly pushed back his chair and then followed her to the pool. She was the first one in, making him 'the rotten egg'. He didn't mind though. He loved to make her laugh.

Chapter Twenty-Three

Later, after the crowd had started to thin out, Lance and Stormy headed back to their room to change out of their swimsuits. Once there, they showered and got ready for bed.

"That was something seeing that matching earring in Nancy's bag," Stormy said to Lance as he sat at the desk, typing on his laptop. "Nancy acted like she'd never seen that earring before, and I hope that's the truth. But did you see the look on Kim's face as she hurried her sister away from our table? I wonder what it was that Kati was going to say. It was as if Kim didn't want her to finish the sentence."

"Yes, now that you mention it," he said, "it sure did. I'll put this incident about the earring in both Nancy's and Kim's file on here for you. Okay?"

"Yes, do that for me, please," Stormy answered. "I think it may add one more piece to this puzzle of ours."

Before Stormy could turn off her cell phone for the night, Detective Marshall called to ask her a few questions. After a brief conversation with him, she turned off her phone and plugged it in for the night to recharge.

"What was that all about?" Lance asked, looking up from his keyboard.

"The detective wanted to know what I knew about Nancy, but I really didn't know much more about her than he did. I mentioned the sea horse earring to him, and he's going to follow up on that with the museum.

"I guess he has reason to wonder about her."

"Yes, he might at that, Stormy replied."

Finishing typing all the information in, Lance suggested that they sit outside on the balcony for a while before retiring for the night. "This may be the last time we get to sit out here and enjoy this view. It's so peaceful."

"Yes, I wish we had a nice balcony at home like this one," Stormy said, gazing out over the city of Austin. "Maybe we could add one onto our house sometime."

"I think that would be nice," Lance said, laughing, "but we'd need to build a second story onto our home in Phoenix first."

"Hey, that would be a great idea," Stormy said, enthusiastically. "When do we start?"

"Oh, what have I gotten myself into now," Lance groaned, looking up at the sky.

* * *

During the night, Stormy found herself suddenly awakened. She had been dreaming of how she and Lance had built a second story onto their home, just to have a fire rage through the place and destroy it all. She was

The Austin Fires

glad to be out of that dream, but unsure of why she had awakened at this late hour.

Then she heard it; a low scraping noise, then a heavy clunking sound. It was the same sounds she had heard those other nights. She was very sure of this.

"I better check this out and see what it is once and for all," Stormy said in a low whisper.

Her curiosity fully aroused, she threw back the sheets and slipped out of bed. She remembered that she had made Lance a promise not to go running off into the night without waking him first, but she was just going to peek out the door and see what was going on.

Certainly this would still be in keeping with that promise, and if I see any one, or feel like I need to go dashing off, I'll come back and wake Lance up first, she thought, stepping to the chair beside the bed.

Throwing on her bathrobe and slippers, she grabbed her walking stick and hurried to the door. Opening it as quietly as she could manage, she looked out into the hallway. She was momentarily startled to see a man kneeling down near the wall a few doors away from her. He was dressed in a dark navy pair of pants with a lighter blue shirt. The hotels' logo was written across his shirt. The man was so intent on what he was doing, he didn't see Stormy poke her head out of the door, then pull it in just as quickly.

She waited behind the closed door for a few more minutes, her heart beating wildly. Carefully opening the door once again, she took another look down the hallway. The man had now risen to his feet and was walking away from her in the direction of the stairs.

She paused until she heard the stairwell door open and then close again before she stepped out into the hallway. Forgetting her promise, she looked around, and seeing no one in the hall, she slowly crept down to where she had seen the man crouching down. There on the wall, just a few inches from the carpeted floor was an air vent with an old-fashioned grating across it. Leaning her walking stick against the wall near her, she crouched down to get a better look at the grate.

She examined it and saw that there were four screws holding it in place against the wall. Looking closer, she saw that one of the screws was slightly out of the wall as if it had been carelessly inserted.

What was that man doing down here by this old grating? She wondered. *I'll bet that if I can get this grate off of the wall, I'll find some answers.*

She stood up and was about to head back to her room in search of something to use to remove the screws, when she discovered that she had put the nail file she had been using earlier on her nails into the side pocket of her robe. Drawing the file out of the pocket and kneeling down by the grating, Stormy attempted to use the blunt end of the nail file in the head of the screw that was part way out. It worked and she soon had it out of the wall and in her hand. Laying it on the carpet below the vent, and looking around the hall, she quickly went to work on the second screw.

Soon she had all four screws out of the grate. Very carefully she lifted it from out of the wall. In doing so, the grate scraped against the wall making the same noise that Stormy had heard from her room. She set one of the

The Austin Fires

grate's ends down on the carpet and leaned the other up against the wall below her.

"Wow, so this is what I was hearing those other nights," she softly said to herself. "Now, let me see if there's anything in here and if I can discover what that man was up to."

Bending down as far as she could, she peered into the vent. It was dark inside and at first, she couldn't see a thing. As her eyes started to adjust, she saw the outline of some sort of metal object. Carefully reaching into the vent, she withdrew the object and pulled it out into the dim light of the hallway. Examining the object, she found it to be a pair of needle nose pliers.

"I wonder what these are doing in here?" she said. "Maybe there are more items back inside."

Reaching carefully in once again, her hand hit another solid object. Grabbing hold of it, she pulled it from the vent to discover another tool, a long flat head screwdriver. Following this, she pulled out a small jar of honey.

Growing ever more puzzled, Stormy continued to search inside the vent. Her fingertips hit an object that felt like plastic to the touch. She almost had it, when it slipped farther back out of her grasp all together.

How am I ever going to get that out of there? She thought.

Then it came to her. She reached over and grabbed her walking stick. She had used it many times to reach the shoeboxes off high department store shelves and to pull things out of places where they had fallen under, so why not inside a vent.

Carefully maneuvering the stick around, she managed to reach the small plastic object and pull it forward to the front of the opening. She reached in and withdrew it. In her hand she found herself holding a small plastic zip lock style bag. Inside the bag was an assortment of miscellaneous items one might find in their pants pockets or purse. She found it contained a piece of string, a tissue, a couple of packets of hotel labeled sugar, a small vial of liquid, and two sticks of chewing gum among some other smaller items.

Why on earth would any one put these things inside of a wall vent? Stormy wondered.

Then she remembered that the man had on a Drakeston Hotel shirt.

He must be one of the hotels' workmen, and for some reason he stores his things here in this vent.

Stormy found this very odd but thought that maybe he had his things stolen before and wanted to find a place to keep them safe. Or maybe he was a kleptomaniac and hid his stolen items in this vent.

"I'd better put these things back before someone comes along and sees me down here on the floor," she said, softly.

She replaced the items as best she could in the same spots she had found them. Lifting the grate from off the floor, she carefully put it back in its place on the wall. It once again made the loud clunking noise as it dropped into place. Now Stormy was positive that this was the sound she'd heard.

Quickly screwing each of the four screws in with her nail file, she made sure all of them were tightly in. She grabbed her stick and stood up.

Looking around the hallway, Stormy hurried back to her room. She entered and quietly closed and locked the

The Austin Fires

door behind her. She was relieved to find that Lance was still asleep. Silently crossing the room, she took off her robe and slippers and carefully slipped under the sheets. She would have to think over this new development before mentioning it to Lance.

Besides telling him I left the room again without awakening him!

Chapter Twenty-Four

"It's a gorgeous morning here in the city of Austin, folks," Clint said, as the group sat around the hotel's café enjoying another wonderful meal. "As you know, this will be our last full day of the tour. Tomorrow we catch the flight back to Dallas/Ft. Worth and the tour ends there, with all of you going on your separate ways. This morning we have a tour lined up at the Capital Building, then on to lunch."

"That sounds like fun," Kim chimed in.

"I think you'll like it," Clint continued. "After lunch, you're all free to do some last minute shopping around the city. Then we'll meet back here at seven o'clock and go to one of the local clubs for a nice dinner. We'll be entertained by one of the great jazz bands on tour here in Austin this week. I think we have a great day planned for you, and we hope you'll all enjoy it."

Clint sat back down at the table to finish the rest of his meal.

S. A. Slack

Having finished their breakfast and dashed back to their rooms for last minute items, the group met outside of the Drakeston to board the van. They found however, that the van was no where to be found, thus making for a nervous and slightly angry Clint.

"I'm sorry for the delay, folks. The new driver they're sending out today doesn't seem as reliable as the old one was." Clint paced back and forth along the hotel's front side walk. "He should have been here waiting for us when we came out. It's too bad that our regular driver came down sick."

"We're okay waiting out here," Stormy reassured him in an attempt to calm him down. "I'm sure he will be here any minute."

As if on cue, the big van pulled up to a stop in front of them. A bearded driver made his apologies to Clint, said something about the stupid drivers on the road today, and the group all climbed into the van. In a matter of minutes, they were off to visit the Capital Building.

When they arrived at their destination, Clint addressed the group.

"We've arranged for you to have a very knowledgeable guide from the Capital take you around this morning. Afterwards, he will take you over to the Governors' Mansion for an interesting tour of that, as well," Clint said, looking at his wrist watch. "I'll join up with you later, as I still have a few last minute arrangements to make. I hope you all have a great time here. They're all yours, Mr. Williams."

Clint left the group, jumping into the waiting van before Stormy could question him about what kind of arrangements he had to make.

The Austin Fires

As Mr. Williams led the group inside the building, she turned to Lance and whispered, "There goes Clint, running off again. I wonder what he had to do this time that was so urgent."

"I do not know, but maybe it was the lunch reservations again," Lance suggested. "He doesn't seem very organized for a tour guide. Maybe that's why he doesn't work for that other agency any longer."

"Maybe so," Stormy wondered.

"The city of Austin was chosen as the capital of the Republic of Texas in 1839, and it became the permanent capital of Texas in the year 1870," the guide began. "You may have heard the slogan here that 'everything is bigger in Texas'? Well, as you look around at our Capitol building, you can see that this phrase rings true. It stands a good three hundred and nine feet tall and was patterned after our nation's Capitol building in Washington D.C., but this building is taller than the one in Washington." The guide pointed toward the ceiling. "It was designed," he continued, "by the great architect, Elijah E. Myers and built of the red granite you see from this area. This building took over seven years to finish and the final price tag for the project was more than three million dollars. You can imagine what that would have been in 1888. The beautiful gardens outside add to the ambiance of the place, which we will go out and see in a short while. Now let's go on to the next room. Follow me this way please."

"This is quite a nice building," Lance said, looking around the room. "I wasn't sure about coming here today, but so far I like it."

"Yes, it is interesting," Stormy said, looking at a display about Texas tourism and the Capital building. "Other than Clint, all the rest of the group seems to be staying together. So far, no one has wandered off or lagged behind."

"And, most of all," Lance said, "no one has started any fires today."

"So far. Let's just hope that it stays that way, and that no one gets injured either," Stormy said. "I would just like a quiet, peaceful time today."

"Let's take a look at the beautiful grounds around the Capital," the guide said, heading toward a pair of glass doors, "and then we'll go and tour the Capital's Visitors Center. It has great historical significance of its own, as you'll see."

The group filtered out into the beautiful gardens surrounding the Capital building and the visitor's center. The guide pointed out the Governor's Mansion and told them that they would go and see that later. Lovely flowers filled the gardens along with, bright green bushes and plants, and the most luscious lawns they had ever seen. There were statues of famous people and several benches to rest on throughout the area.

Stormy noticed that the whole group pretty much continued to follow the guide around the gardens, listening to his speech as they went along. She did notice, however, that Kim and Kati did a lot of hushed talking between themselves throughout the tour, and it appeared to be serious from the looks on their faces.

When they finally reached the visitor's center, the guide explained, "As the Texas General Land Office Building, this is the city's oldest surviving state office structure. It

The Austin Fires

often reminds visitors of the ancient medieval castles by the way it's constructed. In a minute, we'll stop and visit the gift shop in case any of you would like to pick up some souvenirs to take home, but first I'd like to show you this room over here."

He steered them through a door and into a fascinating area filled with a large antique desk, several pens, paintings, books, and many other interesting objects.

"Have you ever heard of Austin described as 'The City of the Violet Crown'? Do you know why it was called that? It was named that by the writer, William Sydney Porter in 1894 in the book he wrote called *Tictocq, The Great French Detective*, in Austin. If you look around, you'll see copies of his books, and over there is the famous stair case he wrote into one of his earlier books. You'll see that as a writer he was called 'O. Henry'."

"Look at what this says about Porter, Stormy," Lance said, reading from a plaque near him. "He was born in North Carolina. William Sydney Porter is better known as O. Henry. He came to Austin, Texas in 1884. In addition to jobs as a clerk, bookkeeper, draftsman, and bank teller, he acted in local theatrical productions and began publishing a weekly newspaper."

"So that's who O. Henry was," Stormy said. "This is all quite fascinating."

"Okay, let's take a few minutes to look around the gift shop now," the guide said, after he had given the group some time to look around the room. He led the way out of another door and into the gift shop. They all found many interesting things to purchase.

"Lance, do you think this pig holding a sign of Texas would be a good gift for our friend, Debbie?" Stormy asked. "She was so nice to volunteer to watch our house and the dog and cats while we're away. You know how much she loves pigs, and this would look great in her collection."

"Yes," Lance agreed, "I think she might like it. And look, I found a couple of new spoons of Texas for your spoon collection. Do you like this one or this other one?"

Stormy chose the smaller headed spoon as it would match her collection size more closely, even if Texas did made everything bigger.

After everyone had chosen a few gifts from the shop, they left and headed for the Governor's Mansion.

"The Governor's Mansion is one of the most historical houses in Texas," the guide remarked. It was built in 1856 and is the oldest continuously occupied executive residence west of the Mississippi, as well as a National Historic Landmark. It has a lot of history to it, but instead of me telling all of it to you, let's tour the mansion and its many guides will explain about each individual area we visit."

They all enjoyed the mansion and had fun asking the guides their many different questions. It was a fun way to learn about Texas history, such as when Texas became a state, problems with Mexican troops, when and what the mansion was used for through out its history, and a variety of other things.

It was not until near the end of the tour that Clint rejoined the group .

"How're you all doing?" he asked, looking around at the mansion walls. "This is a favorite part of the tour for me when I come here to Austin."

The Austin Fires

"So I wonder why he was not here earlier to accompany us," Lance whispered to Stormy.

"I wonder what he really was doing while we were here without him," she mused.

The tour came to an end and thanking their guide, the group headed back to the parking lot of the Capital Building to find their van and go to lunch. Clint told them he had chosen a Tex-Mex place down the road a piece where the food and atmosphere were great.

Chapter Twenty-Five

They arrived at the restaurant and were soon seated. There had been several people ahead of them waiting for a table, and Stormy could see the frustration and impatience on their faces.

I might be upset too if I'd waited a long time and a whole group of people were let in before me that had only just arrived, Stormy thought, fighting the urge to look back at them and apologize.

Soon they were seated, had placed their orders, and were served piping hot plates of food.

"This place is pretty nice," Frank said, shouting above the lively Mexican music. "The food's pretty good, all except for this tamale. It's a little dry. They need some better sauce for it."

"Hey Frank, did you see that display of trains over in the corner of the Capital building?" Lance asked him, swallowing a bite of his sour cream enchilada. "It was pretty cool."

"I sure did," Frank bellowed, putting the last piece of a sopapilla dripping with honey, into his mouth. "It was the best display in the whole place."

"Do you think he would miss a thing like that," Nancy said, reaching for her second sopapilla. "Pass the honey down this way, Stormy, will you?"

"Sure," Stormy said, handing over the container. "I think there were quite a few interesting things to see in all three places we went to today. I hope Lance and I will have a chance to come back and see more of Austin some time. There are so many other places I would've liked to have seen."

"It seems like there's never enough time to visit all of the great places that a city or country has to offer when you visit them," Clint chimed in from where he sat at a nearby table.

"The Bio that Texas' Great Tours sent us about you, along with all of the brochures and papers for the trip," Stormy said, "stated that you had only been with them for about a year. It said that you worked for a different company before them. Why, may I ask, did you switch companies?"

"Oh, well that's kind of a long story," he said, "but needless to say, the boss and I didn't see eye to eye on a few things about tours. So I decided to, uh, leave and find employment elsewhere. I like Texas' Great Tours, and so far they've been good to work for."

"Well, that's good," Lance said. "We all wish you a great and long career with them."

"Thank you," Clint said, a half smile forming on his face.

The Austin Fires

A group of Mexican mariachis struck up a tune, and several Mexican dancers twirled throughout the tables, their skirts flaring outward as they danced to the beat of the music. They all had a great time watching the show and enjoyed their lunch time tremendously.

After they had finished, the group headed out to the van and were driven back to the hotel. Some of them opted to go out shopping for the rest of the afternoon, while others enjoyed a cool dip in the pool or a workout in the gym.

"Hey, Lance," Stormy said when they were alone in the hotel lobby, "why don't we go to the Mall and look around at all the stores there? Clint said we could have the van take us any where in the city we might want to go."

"Okay," Lance agreed, "that sounds like fun. I'll go ask Clint to set it up for us."

Soon they were on their way in the tour's hired van. The same replacement driver that had driven the group that morning was driving them now. He didn't say much to them as they left the hotel and headed down the street.

The traffic on Austin's streets was fairly busy that afternoon, but they made much better time as soon as they hit the highway. Lance asked the driver if he might turn on the radio, and after selecting a station, they sat back and enjoyed the music. It was a very enjoyable ride, but as they neared their destination, Stormy once again thought she smelled smoke.

"Oh no, not again. Not another fire!"

"Its definitely smells like it," Lance said, sniffing the air, "but not really a fire, more like oil or fluid burning. Hey, driver…"

They had just reached the intersection leading to the mall and were approaching a red stop sign. Instead of coming to a halt, the van sped up and ran right through it, narrowly missing the cross traffic. Even though Lance and Stormy had on their seat belts, they were violently tossed around as the van sped down a row of parked cars.

A vehicle, backing out of a parking space, slammed on its brakes just in time to avoid being hit by the run away van. Arriving at the end of the parking row, the van skidded around the corner, slamming up against the curb and bouncing off again. The curb had slowed their speed, but the van kept on moving. Up ahead, a mother and her two small children had just entered a cross walk. Stormy was sure they were going to hit them, but from the wild honking of the van's driver on the horn, the mother was able to see them coming, and she pulled her children out of the way just in time.

The van continued to race through the parking lot. Lance and Stormy noticed that their driver was attempting to stop the vehicle by pumping the brakes repeatedly, but to no avail. He continued to honk the horn furiously as he tried to slow the van, shifting its gears down as people and other vehicles barely got out of its' way.

Finally, the van veered off to the right, went up over the curb and onto the sidewalk, skimming the side of the van on a large gray lamp post. The vehicle scraped loudly along the post, coming to a stop just inches before reaching the side of the Mall's stone wall.

The Austin Fires

The trio sat there for a few moments, dazed at their narrow escape from serious injury, or possibly worse. When they finally came to their senses and looked out the windows, they saw that a crowd was starting to gather around them, and a few of the men were reaching over and trying to open the doors of the van.

The doors along the van's left side were damaged and could not be opened due to the damage from the pole. A man was just asking if he could help those inside, when a Mall Security truck pulled up, sirens blaring. A fire truck could be heard off in the distance.

"You all right, ma' am?" one of the big burly security men said to Stormy. "Did you get hurt?"

"No, I think I'm alright," she answered. "I'm just a little shook up, that's all. How about you Lance?'

"I'm okay," Lance said, holding a blood soaked hand with his other one. "My hand just hurts a little."

"Oh, Lance. You'd better have that looked at," Stormy said, concern in her voice. "We need to get that bleeding stopped right away."

Taking several tissues from out of the purse she had retrieved from off the floor, Stormy wrapped them tightly around Lances' hand. Just then, a fire truck pulled up and several firefighters jumped down from the truck, including two paramedics. They hurried toward the van and began asking questions as they extracted all three of the group from the vehicle.

They checked them over and found that not only did Lance's hand need treating, but their driver had a nasty cut across his forehead.

"Are you alright, Mrs. Winters?" a voice behind Stormy asked. Turning around, she saw that it was Capt. Smith who had addressed her.

"Oh hi, Captain," Stormy replied, recognizing the fireman. "Yes, I'm alright, just a bit shook up, but Lance cut his hand up when the van hit that pole. He was on the side of the van that took the hit."

"I'm sorry to hear that, but I'm glad to see that none of you were injured any worse ," the Captain said. "I talked with the driver, and he said that the brakes just gave out. He said they seemed a little soft when on the highway, but not too bad until he got off the highway and approached that stop sign."

"I wonder what happened to the brakes," Stormy asked, as she looked back to see the paramedic bandaging Lance's hand. "We were all out in it this morning and it seemed just fine then."

"We'll have it towed to the garage, and it'll be thoroughly gone through," he said. "Would you like a ride back to the hotel? I'm going that way."

"I'd really wanted to see the mall here," she said, "but considering what has happened, I think we'd better take you up on your offer."

Lance arose from the back of the paramedic's truck where he'd been sitting and walked over to where Stormy and the Captain stood. He insisted that he was fine and could walk around the shopping mall with Stormy.

"No, you will not." she told him in no uncertain terms. "We're going back to the hotel with Captain Smith here."

She got Lance into the Captain's car and they returned back to the hotel.

The Austin Fires

After thanking Capt. Smith for his help, Stormy led Lance into the hotel, onto the elevator, and up to their room. She insisted that he lie down for a while and rest before it was time to go to the club that night.

"Maybe we should forget about the club tonight and just have a quiet dinner in our room," Stormy suggested to Lance.

"No, I'll be fine, dear," Lance said, resting his head on two fluffy pillows with his feet up on the bed. "I think it'll be alot of fun at the club, and Clint said something about a jazz singer. After all, this is our last night here in Austin."

"Well, okay. It would be fun," Stormy said, lying down next to him on the bed. "I think I'll rest my legs for awhile until it's time to go."

Chapter Twenty-Six

"Here we are folks," Clint said, later that evening, as their replacement van pulled up outside of the 'Pomegranate Lounge'. "This is one of the best places for Jazz singers in all of Austin. We also have a great meal planned for you, so let's go inside. I hope you'll all enjoy yourselves."

The group entered the palm tree covered entrance and made their way past the many large potted ferns in the entryway to the main part of the restaurant. The lights, which hung over each table, had been turned down low to create a romantic atmosphere about the place. Bright stars, painted against a dark blue background on the ceiling overhead, made one feel as if they were sitting at tables under a starry sky. Winding their way around the many pomegranate trees placed about, they were led to tables covered with soft white tablecloths and beautiful dinnerware near the middle of the large room.

"Wow, what a great place this is," Amy said, her eyes aglow as she looked over the room before she sat down in the chair Tom held out for her. "I'm glad that Clint told us to wear our best clothes for this occasion."

"Me, too," Stormy said.

She was glad she had thought to bring her nice aqua-colored evening dress with her when she had packed, and that she had insisted on Lance bringing one of his good suits, as well.

"Thank you, Lance," she said, as he held her chair for her. "Be careful with that hand, dear. I don't want to see you injure it further."

"Don't worry, it's feeling much better already."

"That may be due to the heavy pain medication that paramedic gave you," Stormy said, smiling.

"That helps a lot when my old back gets to hurting," Frank said. "It gets worse with age I'm afraid. Right, Nancy?"

"Well, for some of us anyway, Frank," she replied to her husband. "Others of us are just in better shape than some."

"Hey," Frank said, feigning hurt.

"She got you there, old boy," Tom said. "You know, as we age we have to take even better care of ourselves. We need to continue to exercise every day and watch what we eat. It helps to learn to relax a bit each day, too, and it will help get some of the stress out of our lives."

"And take two aspirin and call him in the morning," Amy laughed, looking over at Tom with a mischievous grin on her face.

Tom looked over at her and was about to say something, but thought better of it.

The Austin Fires

"I think that's very good advice, Tom," Stormy said. "I know that I always feel much better when I eat right and exercise regularly. Lance and I have been trying to do better with these things over the last few years. It's made a big difference in our lives."

"Yes, it has," Lance said, a sparkle in his eye. "I just don't mention what I have to eat for lunch when I am out running errands some days."

"You don't have to," she said to him, "when you forget and leave the wrappers on the seat of the car."

The group broke out in laughter.

Their waiter soon arrived with a large tray, and they were all served a wonderful looking salad topped with red onions and miniature croutons. In addition, he placed a few baskets of fresh homemade rolls with sides of honey butter on the table.

After they had finished their salads, their waiter brought them each a plate containing a large slice of roast beef, a baked potato with sour cream and chives on top, and a mixture of steamed vegetables.

As they were eating their meal, the restaurant's manager came forward and stood in front of a small stage not far from them. He brought the microphone he held in one hand up to his mouth and introduced the program for the night. As the audience applauded, the curtains opened up on a small jazz band starting their show off with a very lively tune. After a couple of songs, the curtains behind them parted and a man came forth and burst into song.

"Oh, Kim," Katie shouted out over the music. "Look who it is! Did you ever think we'd get to see him in person?"

"No, I didn't," Kim replied, an excited look on her face. "Wait until I tell my husband about this. He'll wish he could've been here, too."

The show continued as the singer sang his way through several more pieces. Finally he bowed to the applause, promising to return later on in the evening, and left the stage the way he had come in through the curtains behind him. The jazz band continued on with their music with the manager once again taking his microphone to suggest that the diners do a little dancing in the cleared area near the stage.

Tom asked Amy if she would like to dance and away they went out on the dance floor. Stormy was surprised to see how well both Amy and Tom could dance. Together they flowed as one as the music played about them.

When the musicians slowed down the music, Lance asked Stormy to join him on the dance floor. She was careful of his injured hand.

The sisters, Kim and Kati, sat back at the table enjoying the music and watching the others dance the night away. Clint asked them each to come and dance with him, and not wanting to hurt his feelings, they consented to one dance each.

It was getting quite late in the night when they all arrived back at the hotel. The van dropped them off out front and they headed inside. Tonight, not one of them suggested stopping at the café for ice cream. They all went up in the elevator together to their floor and on to their separate rooms, wishing each other a good night's sleep.

"Tonight was a lot of fun," Stormy said, removing her earrings and placing them in the rolled cloth she always carried them in. "Lance, if I hold this side of the necklace,

The Austin Fires

could you help me with the clasp. Please be careful not to hurt your hand."

"Sure. I had a lot of fun, too," Lance agreed, unclasping the necklace. "I think it was a great way to spend our last night here in Austin. I'm glad that our return flight is later in the morning tomorrow. It'll give us a chance to get a good night's rest."

Chapter Twenty-Seven

Later, in the dark of night, a lone figure crept slowly down the hallway careful not to make any loud noises that might wake someone up. It carried a small bag in one hand and made its way to stand in front of the grate in the wall not far from the Winters' door. Setting the bag on the hallway carpeting below the grate, it quickly and carefully removed the grate, leaning it against the hall wall. It quietly removed the contents inside the vent and placed them in the bag. Just as carefully, it replaced the grate back into the wall. Taking the bag, it headed for the stairs and disappeared through the stairwell door.

Stormy and Lance, tired from the days events, heard nothing of the hallway visitor, sleeping right through it's' visit.

A short while later, if they had been out on their balcony enjoying the night, they would have seen a figure climbing up the fire escape below to one of the hotel's nearby windows. The figure quickly and stealthily made its way to the window. Withdrawing an object from a small bag, it inserted the object into the window that had been left open a tiny, unnoticeable crack and quietly pried it upward. Pulling out a small vial of liquid and removing the top, the figure reached an arm in through the window and quickly emptied the vial's liquid onto a small pile of white sugar like substance on the carpet below. A sudden poof sounded and flames shot up, licking hungrily at the bottom of the window's heavy drapes.

Withdrawing its arm, the figure quickly took out a small packet from the same bag, and squeezed its contents out across the windowsill, closing the window tightly over it. It put the empty items back into the bag and hurried down the fire escape.

Dropping to the pavement below, it ran around the corner of the hotel and disappeared into a side entrance of the hotel, which had been propped open by the use of a piece of wood.

During the night, Stormy dreamed again about being in a fire. In the dream, she and Lance were caught in a burning building as the flames raged throughout it, room by room. The smoke was so thick that she had lost sight of Lance and began calling out his name.

"What's a matter, Stormy?" Lance said, shaking his wife's arm as she lay next to him in bed. "Wake up, it's okay."

"Lance," Stormy said, now fully awake, "you're alright! Oh, that was an awful dream. I dreamt that our house was burning and I couldn't find you any where."

"It was just a dream, and as you can see, I'm okay." Lance pulled her into his strong arms. "Maybe a drink of water would make you feel better. I'll go and get you one."

The Austin Fires

"No, that's okay," Stormy said, disengaging from his arms and sitting up. "I need to get something for the headache I have anyway."

She got out of bed and headed for the bathroom. While in there, she was sure she smelled smoke.

Oh, that's silly, she chided herself, *it must be left over from my dream.*

Being rather sleepy, she headed back to bed when she was finished. Upon reaching the bed, she stopped and sniffed the air around her. She was sure that the scent of smoke hung heavily in the air. Then, from out of nowhere, she heard what sounded like a muffled scream.

"What was that?" Lance said, opening his eyes. He had dozed off while his wife had been in the bathroom.

"It sounded like a scream from a room down the hall," Stormy said as she hurriedly put on her robe and slippers. "I definitely smell smoke coming from the hallway." Grabbing her walking stick, she headed in the direction of the door.

"You're right. I can smell it, too," Lance said, jumping up from the bed and grabbing his robe and shoes. "Wait for me and we'll check it out together."

Stormy waited as he put on his shoes and then flung open the door and rushed out into the hallway. Looking down the hall, they saw small wisps of smoke coming from under Amy's door. They hurried toward her room, and Lance banged on the door.

"Amy, are you okay?" Stormy yelled through the door.

When there was no reply, Lance tried the doorknob. It would not even budge, so he tried using an old football move to break it loose. He stepped back from the door, and lowering his body down, he ran at it. His body rammed into the wooden door with a thud, but the door continued to hold fast.

"What's going on out here?" Kim said from the open door across the hallway. Seeing the smoke, she cried back over her shoulder, "Katie, come quickly! There's smoke coming from Amy's room."

"Katie appeared in the doorway and pushed her way in front of Kim. "Is Amy in there? Is she alright?"

"We don't know, but if she is, we need to get her out of there now," Stormy yelled. "Call hotel security and tell them there's a fire up here and someone may be trapped. Hurry!"

"I know what we can use to open this door," Lance said, drawing Stormy attention in his direction as he dashed down the hall. "There's a fire extinguisher on the wall."

Reaching the red-trimmed case, he broke the glass and pulled out the container. Running back down the hall, he returned to Amy's door.

"Is that strong enough to break down a door?" Stormy questioned him.

"I don't know, but we're about to find out," he replied, "It's quite heavy, and you hear about people using it this way, so I'm going to give it a try." He pulled back the fire extinguisher in his two hands and hit the doorknob area of the door with it as hard as he could. "A-h-h-h!" he yelled out in pain as the container made contact with the door. The door latch gave way a little, but did not break open.

"Oh, Lance!" Stormy cried out. "Your poor hand. It's bleeding again." The bandage on his injured hand sported a bright red spot on it. "Let's try something else instead." She looked around the hall and spotted a maid's cart at one end. "Kim, run down and grab that cart, and bring it back here as fast as you can. Amy's life may depend on us!"

Kim, joined by her sister, Katie, ran as fast as they could to the end of the hall, their open bathrobes flowing out behind them. They quickly covered the distance, grabbed the cart, and whisked it back to where Stormy stood waiting. A few other doors along the hall had opened at the noise, and Kim and Kati yelled out a warning to them about the fire. The occupants of those rooms ran back inside to get their things and leave the floor in search of a safer place.

"Oh, the front desk said for all of us to leave this floor as quickly as we can," Kati said. "They're calling the fire station and sending up security to get Amy out. But we're not going to just leave her like this!"

"It may be too late by the time they can get up here," Stormy said, looking over the maid's cart. "I think we need to keep trying. This cart looks pretty strong, so I think we can use it to ram the door and break it down."

"Stand back, Storm," Lance said, grabbing onto the cart's handle, more blood showing forth on his bandaged hand.

"Not alone you won't," she said, holding a hand up to him. "Not with that hand. Look at it. Girls, give us a hand with this"

She removed four large towels from the maid's cart and threw them over one of her arms. Then she grabbed on tightly to the end of the cart, getting ready to push.

"We're ready," Kim said, stepping forward beside Stormy.

"Definitely," Katie replied, along side her sister.

"Okay, here we go. Give it all you have," Lance yelled out. "One, two, three, push!"

The four of them pushed the cart into the door as hard as they could. The door flew open and heavy smoke poured out into the corridor. Just then, Frank emerged from his room down the hall, as several more guests came from theirs, wondering what was going on.

Quite a large crowd had now gathered in the hallway. As the rest watched, several others headed for the elevator to escape the disaster.

"What's going on?" Frank yelled down the hall, hurrying toward Army's room and the broken door.

Not stopping to wait for Frank, Stormy threw Lance and each of the sisters a towel. Covering her own mouth and nose with the one she still held, she headed into the smoke filled room. Frank arrived at the door as the two sisters hesitated.

"Wait here," Lance commanded. "I'll go in with my wife to look for Amy." With that, he dashed into the room.

"Let me see that towel young lady," Frank demanded of Kim.

Kati moved back from the door and out of his way, while Kim gingerly handed over her towel. Frank disappeared into the smoke.

Once inside, Stormy's eyes filled with tears, and she couldn't see a thing through the thick smoke that filled the room. An intense heat shot through her body from the nearby fire, while a burning sensation crawled across

The Austin Fires

the surface of her skin. She was grateful that she had remembered to bring her walking stick with her. Using the end of it, she felt her way through the smoke. She was glad that she had been in Amy's room the day of the intruder, and that she remembered where the furniture had been placed. This room had been laid out differently from the one she and Lance occupied.

Navigating through the smoke, and heading in the direction of what she hoped was the bed and away from the fire, she heard Lance's voice call out to her.

"I'm over here," she yelled back, hoping he could hear her over the roar of the burning fire. The heat of the flames creeping along the room's wall made her feel faint, but the fires' light helped to illuminate the bed as she drew closer to it. There, on the bed, Stormy made out the form of a person. It lay there as still as could be.

This must be Amy, she thought, as she neared the bed.

She reached down and carefully turned over the form, relieved to see that it was indeed Amy. Just then, Lance, followed by Frank, appeared out of the smoke, stepping to the opposite side of the bed. They were holding the towels over their faces.

"Here she is, Lance," Stormy shouted at the men, briefly removing the towel from her own face, "but she doesn't seem to be conscious, and I can't tell if she's breathing at all."

"Let's just get her out of this room. We'll take it from there," Lance shouted back over the bed. He and Frank tied their towels behind their heads the best they could and picked up the limp girl. As they headed for the door,

Lance shouted to Stormy, "Follow us out, Storm. Stay close behind me as we go."

Stormy started to hurry around the bed to follow after them, when she spotted a purse lying on a chair next to the bed.

She'll need this purse and it'll just take a minute to retrieve it, Stormy thought as she turned and headed for the chair.

Picking up the purse, she turned back to leave. She had taken a few steps when the intense heat of the fire made her feel woozy. Grabbing onto the edge of the table, she stood there for a minute, steadying herself. As she stood, her dream came flooding back into her mind of the house fire where she and Lance had been separated. A heavy feeling of fear and panic shot through her, making her feel all the weaker.

No, Stormy, she thought, chiding herself, *stop thinking about that. You have to keep moving. You have to get out of here. Go, now!*

Forcing herself to move, Stormy used her walking stick to feel her way back through the smoke filled room as the flames continued burning.

She was half way across the room, making her way to the door, when she felt someone near her side. Raising her stick above her head, she got ready to strike out, when a person shouted, "There you are. I thought you were right behind us."

Through the smoke Lance's face appeared. Stormy was overjoyed as she saw her husband. Never had she seen such a beautiful sight.

"Let's get you out here before you collapse," he said to her, a concerned look on his face.

The Austin Fires

"Yes, we'd better leave," Stormy said, lowering her stick and taking his arm. "I'll be fine once we're out of here. You know, I almost hit you with my stick, you startled me so."

"Well, I am glad you didn't," he grinned back at her. "It would've made it a little hard to rescue you."

It was not until then that Stormy heard the sound of the spray coming from the fire extinguishers being aimed at the flames. As they neared the door, she saw Frank and another man she had not seen before, attempting to put out the fire before it spread any further. The man told Lance that he was from the Drakeston's Hotel security, and that the fire trucks would be here at any moment.

Once outside the room and back into the hallway, Stormy was relieved to be out of the smoke. She found that she could both breathe and see much better. Most of all, she was glad to see that Amy was being attended to. Even though she felt a little weak still, Stormy made her way down the hall, steadying herself with her walking stick, to where Amy lay. Several people were surrounding Amy and when Stormy arrived, she was pleased to see that Kim and Katie had wrapped a blanket around Amy, placed her head on a pillow, and were now wiping her face with a damp cloth.

"How's she doing?" Stormy asked Kim.

"I think she'll be okay," Kim replied, looking up at Stormy from her crouched position on the floor. "She came to for a few minutes and asked for Tom. Nancy was here and volunteered to go find him. Here she comes now."

"I can't find Tom anywhere," Nancy said, a worried look on her face. "I looked in his room when he didn't answer my knocking. I found his door was unlocked and actually open a crack. And no one has seen him at all since we came back from the club."

"Maybe he did this to Amy?" Kati said. "Do you think he would do such a thing to his own fiancé`?"

"I don't know," Stormy said, "but I sure hope not."

She looked around the hall and saw that the elevator was just reaching their floor. The doors opened and out stepped several fire fighters dressed in full fire fighting gear. They headed toward the room where a small amount of smoke still poured forth. Stepping off the elevator behind them was Capt. Smith, along with two paramedics. The elevator doors next to them also opened up, and out stepped a uniformed policeman, followed by Detective Marshall, with the hotel manager behind him.

"Get these people out of here," Captain Smith shouted to the firefighter and hotel manager. "Get them down to the lobby, but don't let them leave. Detective Marshall will be down to question them shortly."

Seeing Amy lying there on the floor, the two paramedics hurried over to help as Captain Smith headed toward Amy's blackened room.

Stormy and the sisters moved out of the way for the Paramedics to do their work, and the crowd of people cleared the hallway and filled the elevator. As they did so, Stormy caught a glimpse of a man looking out from the stairwell. When he noticed that she was looking his way, he quickly shut the door, disappearing from sight.

Chapter Twenty-Eight

Looking down the hall to see where Lance was, and spotting him entering Amy's burned out room with the captain and Detective Marshall, Stormy made a quick decision and headed for the stairs. Arriving at the stairwell, she opened the door and stepped through it. She looked down over the edge of the stairs in time to see the next floors stairwell door swinging shut. Hurrying down the stairs as quickly as she could, she felt her strength renewed as her adrenalin kicked in.

Opening the door, she stepped out into the hall and quickly looked around her. Down at the far end of the hallway, she spotted a second door closing. Quickly making her way down the hall, she arrived at the door. Looking around, and making sure no one was in sight, she leaned against the door, and putting her ear up to it, she listened.

"It's a shame! Your girlfriend is going to live after all," she heard a man's muffled angry voice coming through the door. "You were going to be blamed for her death, but your nosy companions have changed my plans. It's you that's going to die now."

"Not if I have anything to say about it," Stormy whispered to herself. "Sorry, Lance, I know I promised you, but there's no time to wait."

Raising her walking stick up over her head with her right hand, she carefully turned the doorknob with her other. Relieved to find it turned easily in her hand, she opened the door and stepped quietly into the room.

Making her way to the corner of the wall, she stopped and peered around it. A man, with his back turned to her, was standing over someone on the bed who appeared to be bound and gagged.

Oh my, it's Clint, Stormy thought. *Could it have been him all along?*

"If it wasn't for the incompetence of your father," the angry man yelled, "my wife would still be alive. He shouldn't have given her that medication. It only made things worse for her. He killed her, and now it's pay back time."

As the angry man shifted his weight to one side, Stormy had a clear view of the bound figure on the bed. It was Tom! He looked as if he had been roughed up and had a stream of bright red blood running down from a corner of his mouth, his hair a matted mess.

Stormy noticed that Tom was staring intently at the other man's hand, fear in his eyes. Her own eyes were drawn to the man hand as he flung it outward, continuing to yell at Tom. She was shocked to see what the man held in his hand; a very wicked looking knife with about a six inch blade.

The Austin Fires

I've got to stop him from hurting Tom, Stormy thought.

Being short on time to plan her moves, she turned her walking stick upside down, and holding it firmly in her hands, sneaked out from behind the wall and quickly approached the man from behind.

Stepping as stealthily as she could, her movements caught Tom's eye and he looked her way. A look of recognition and then puzzlement passed over his face. The angry man, seeing the look on Tom's face, started to turn in Stormy's direction. Aware of her precarious situation, she knew she must act fast or lose her chance to help Tom and most likely, her own life.

Stormy brought the walking stick down on the side of the man's head as hard as she could. An unexpected rush of adrenalin, flowing through her at that moment, caused her to knock the man sideways toward a nearby chair making him to hit his head and crumple to the floor.

She stood there for a moment in bewilderment, looking at the unconscious form on the floor.

"That's not Clint," she said, confused and surprised at the same time, "but he sure looks alot like him. I wonder who this is?"

A muffled cry, coming from the direction of the bed, shook Stormy from her thoughts and cleared her mind. She headed over to the bed and a much relieved Tom.

It took her a few minutes to untie all of the many knots in the cloth Tom had been bound with, but she finally had him loose and sitting up on the bed.

"Wow! You pack quite a punch with that stick, Mrs. Winters," Tom said, wiping at the running blood from his lower lip. "Thank you for helping me out of this sticky situation. He'd completely lost his mind."

"Yes, I believe he would've killed you," she said, handing him a couple of tissues from a nearby box to hold against his lip. "It's a good thing my husband talked me into buying this solid metal stick when he did, instead of the wooden one I was considering at the time. I think we'd better call security and get them up here right away before he wakes up."

"It looks like he'll by out for a while," Tom said, picking up the ties that had held him and moving over to where the stricken man lay, "but I'll use these to tie him up just in case while you place the call."

Chapter-Twenty-Nine

A grim looking Detective Marshall arrived with the paramedics in tow. He was surprised at the scene he saw before him. Putting this aside, he briefly questioned Tom and Stormy as a paramedic attended to Tom's wounds. Deciding that he would talk further with the two of them at a later time, once he took care of the injured man on the floor, he pulled a radio from his belt and left them.

A stretcher was called for, and as the injured, moaning man was carried from the room, Lance came dashing in through the open door.

"There you are, Stormy," Lance said, relieved to have found her. "I've been searching all over the hotel for you. Are you alright?"

He grabbed her up in a huge embrace and kissed her firmly on the lips. Releasing his hold, he held her at arm's length.

"What am I going to do with you? You keep running off into dangerous situations without telling me where you're going."

"Well..." Stormy began, but Tom interrupted her.

"If she'd waited any longer," Tom said, "and not come to my aid when she did, I would be the one they're carrying out of here, and most likely in a body bag. I owe her my life, Mr. Winters." He went over to Stormy and gave her a quick hug. "If I can ever do anything for you, please call me and it's done. No matter what it is. Now I'd better go and check on Amy." He turned and hurried for the door, stepping from sight.

The police spent the next several hours questioning everyone on the group's floor, and several others in the hotel. The fire had been thoroughly extinguished, and fortunately for the hotel, had not spread to any of the other rooms.

* * *

The tour group sat around several of the tables in the hotel's cafe, eating an early morning breakfast. Since the police had already questioned the group, and they didn't have to leave for the airport for a few more hours yet, they'd decided they might as well eat before packing their things.

"Wow, this has been some trip." Frank said, somewhat quieter than usual. "It was not like I expected it would be."

"No, it's not like any of us had thought it would be, I'm sure," Stormy added, taking a sip of her hot cocoa, "but we've seen some very interesting things here in

Austin. It's a great place to visit, and Lance and I hope to come back again some day."

"Yes, it's a great place," Kim said, then hesitated, looking over at Kati. Kati nodded at Kim. "I have something to tell you. It's about that sea horse earring they found at the fire and the matching one in Nancy's bag. Well, those are mine. I'd lost them some where earlier, as I've told the police. Kati can attest to this."

The group looked startled, all except for Stormy.

"Yes, she did," Kati said, nodding at the others. "I tried to help her find them, but they were no where around. We searched every where."

"When that one turned up near the fire at the museum, and then the other one in Nancy's bag, that must have worried you," Stormy said, looking over at Nancy, then back at Kim. "I guess you were afraid to speak up, thinking you might be blamed for the fire?"

"Yes," Kim said. "I'm sorry about that, Nancy. I should've said something at the time."

"Well, I guess I might have felt the same way if they'd been mine," Nancy replied. "I was worried for a while there that they might blame me for all of this."

At that moment, Clint and Tom walked into the cafe.

"Hi, folks," Clint said, taking a seat at one of the tables. "I hope you're all doing well."

"Yes, we're okay," Lance said, setting his fork down on his empty plate. "Would you join us for breakfast?"

"I'm not hungry right now," Clint said, looking very tired and a bit down. "Maybe later, thanks."

"I think I'll just have a cup of coffee," Tom said. "I'll eat later on, as well."

He went over to a nearby counter and poured himself a cup, returning to sit in a chair beside Stormy.

"How's Amy doing?" she asked Tom. "Will she be able to fly out today with the rest of us?"

"They'd like to keep her over night at the hospital for observation," Tom replied. "But we'd already changed our flight plans last night when I told Amy that I had a surprise for her and that we'd be staying on for a few more days. I arranged with a friend of mine, whose family owns a dude ranch near Austin, to get us a reservation there."

"Ah, that's what that was," Lance remarked, glancing over at Stormy. "My wife saw you talking to someone down in the street the other night when we were out on the balcony."

"Oh, that was my friend, Dave from the ranch I'm talking about," Tom explained, turning toward Stormy. "I didn't want Amy to find out ahead of time, so we had to meet outside. I guess that looked a little funny meeting someone out at night on a dark street, especially with all the fires and strange incidences going on around us, huh."

"Yes, a little bit," Stormy said, laughing. "What about that man that threatened you?" she asked, more seriously. "He sure was angry at you and your father. And attacking Amy the way he did. What happened with his wife, if I may ask?"

"I can answer part of that," Clint said, a sad look coming over his face. "She had a rare disease that was difficult to diagnose. It wasn't Tom's father's fault. He tried everything he could to help her. He even tried a new medication they had just released from some place in Colorado."

"Oh, my husband was on the team that was working on some new medication they recently released," Kim interrupted, "They have big hopes for it. I wonder if it's the same one."

"It may have been," Clint continued. "Her husband is my cousin, the one who attacked you, Tom, and the one, it looks like, that set all these fires. When she died, I guess he went out of his mind. We all thought that he was handling her death okay, accepting it, but I guess we were wrong." Clint looked down at his hands. "I thought he was just being friendly when he asked me questions about our tour here in Austin. He must have found out that you and Amy were coming on this tour, Tom, and hatched a plan to get at your father. It looks like he's been following us all around Austin, trying to cause us trouble. I'm sorry about all of this, folks."

"It's not your fault, Clint," Tom said. "These things just happen. In fact, I've had a few classes on this subject at the University already in my studies. I think I'd like to study it more in depth."

"Well," Clint said, looking around at the group and pulling some papers out of his shirt pocket, "on behalf of the tour group, and myself, we would like to extend to you these coupons for half price on any tours you wish to go on with our group in the future. Texas' Great Tours is affiliated with a few other groups across the country as well, so you can use them in many places."

"Thank you, Clint," Lance said, taking the coupons offered he and Stormy. "Well, I think we'd better go get packed so we'll be ready to go to the airport when it's time."

"Yes," Kati said. "Kim, we'd better hurry too, so we can get that big suitcase of yours closed in time. We may both have to sit on it to get it zipped up with all of those souvenirs we bought on this trip."

They all laughed as they arose and left the café to pack their bags.

"Well, Sherlock," Lance teased her, as they headed for the elevators, "Watson needs a little break. I hope we have an uneventful flight home."

"You never know about airports," Stormy said, a twinkle forming in her eye. "I'd better hang on to this trusty walking stick of mine just in case."

The two of them broke out laughing as they stepped into the waiting elevator.

S. A. Slack, author of children's books as well as mystery novels, brings her characters to life once more in The Austin Fires, A Stormy Winters Mystery. Renowned for her story telling and love of a good mystery, she now finds herself with more tiime for writing after having raised six children. Watch out! It's full speed ahead.

Born in Phoenix, Arizona, she now resides in Texas with her husband and youngest son.

Printed in the United States
90119LV00007B/1-9/A